Sweet Dreams, Doc

Sheri Mizell

Sweet Dreams, Doc

"Sheri did such a great job of bringing a love story to the Lowcountry!"
Wendi Riley

"Sheri, I absolutely loved this story. It is so refreshing to read a love story that truly is about unconditional love. No, life is not perfect but isn't it great to be able to escape to a story where we accept each other without trying to change one another. This was an easy read and you had to finish it once you got started. I loved the characters!!!" **Penny Fender**

"Great read from beginning. This book draws you in and you actually feel as if you can picture the Characters and experience the Southern Charm."
Tammie Jackson

"Absolutely great quick read! Perfect for an afternoon on the beach watching the shrimp boats making their hauls. Beautiful setting on the coast of the S. C. Lowcountry. Beautifully written, tender love story with a quirky twist of fate that shows what total commitment and unconditional love can overcome. A must summer read! Great timing of release with early start of shrimping season in the Lowcountry. A first novel by a small town girl fulfilling a dream of being published whose love of the Lowcountry, the sea, and writing combines to make a truly awesome read." **Cathy Hill**

Sweet Dreams, Doc

To my sons, Evan and Ethan for always believing I could do this, my family for always encouraging me and supporting me, even on my darkest days and for my friends for being patient with me while I lost my mind in the process.

Lastly, to all the men I've loved and hated in my lifetime – thanks for the material.

Sweet Dreams, Doc

This book has been a long time coming, but has been written for quite some time. It all began in the late 1990s as a form of therapy, but after the first few chapters, the characters took on their own lives and I just kept writing and writing. I couldn't wait to find out what happened next.

The accuracy of some terms may not be complete and the Gullah language may be incorrect at times, but I beg forgiveness. I wrote as I heard it…literally, in my head. For those of you who couldn't wait to read it, here it is. I hope I haven't disappointed anyone and I hope you all think it was worth the wait.

I love you all and thank you, from the bottom of my heart, for giving me the push to make this finally possible.

Sweet Dreams, Doc

CHAPTER ONE

Noah Litchfield was standing on the dock observing the goings-on up the hill above the bay. He'd seen those two good-looking gals off and on for several weeks now, but hadn't a clue who they were. Too busy. Too sidetracked by his latest endeavor. One Miss Tracy Murray, the new girl down at the roadhouse.

"Dat be da new doc, Noah," Jasper Hampton informed Noah, patting him on the back.

Jasper was short and chunky, with skin as black as the night. He had worked for the Litchfields for twenty years; Noah had practically grown up with him.

"That so, Jasp? Which one is she?" Noah asked.

"Da pritty 'un. Wid dat long blonde hair,"

Jasper replied with a grin. He knew Noah and his wild ways.

"They both look pretty good to me, old man!" Noah laughed. "Maybe I'll see if she needs some help, welcome her to the neighborhood."

"Noah, one day sum woman gonna make ya scraightun' up!" Jasper laughed.

"Never happen, Jasp," Noah grinned, smoothing back his chestnut hair as he started up the hill.

He picked up a box of photo albums sitting on the back steps and lightly knocked on the door. The blonde one answered the door hesitantly.

"Hi, welcome to Canton Cope. Thought you could use a hand," Noah smiled.

"Oh, thank you . . . and you are?" Maddie questioned as she took the box from his arms.

"I'm sorry. Noah, Noah Litchfield," he apologized, reaching out to shake her hand.

"I'm Maddie Blaylock, Dr. Madison Blaylock" Maddie smiling, turning to the red head, "and this is my friend, Moby Muller." Moby was all but drooling.

"Nice to meet both of you," Noah grinned back at Moby.

"Would you like to come in? Have some lemonade?" Maddie offered.

"Thank you, but no. I've got to get back to the docks. Just wanted to welcome you and tell you if you need anything, my number's in the phone book."

"Well, thank you Noah. I appreciate that," Maddie said.

"Oh yeah, well I hope to see you again,

soon!" Moby melted like butter.

"You ladies have a nice afternoon," Noah called out as he headed back down to the harbor. They watched him as he descended the hill toward the docks enjoying the 'view' from the bay window.

"Gosh, would you look at that back side!" Moby sighed.

"That's one fine man," Maddie agreed. "But did you catch the last name? Litchfield."

"So? What's that mean?"

"Litchfield, as in Litchfield Shrimp. He's probably married with two plus kids, living in a big house somewhere."

"Oh, but Maddie, with a body like that, I'd do some detective work. I gotta know if he's married. What if he's single? Gee . . . single and loaded to boot. I may see if I can't find me a nice little abode up here myself!" Moby giggled.

****

Canton Cope, just up the coast of South Carolina, provided the largest shrimp supply for most of the eastern seaboard than any other. Nearly every family in the small town had someone that worked for Litchfield Shrimp, a father, a brother, a grandfather, or an uncle, practically every man in Canton Cope had worked on a trawler. There was no other industry to be found within 50 miles of the town and with a commodity like shellfish, Litchfield wasn't likely to ever downsize or go out of business.

A job with Kirkland Litchfield was one that you knew you'd keep until the day you retired. Kirkland was an easy man to work for. Polite, well-mannered, understanding and patient, he treated his employees like family and in return, they worked their souls to the bone for him. He was close to seventy years old, and ready to retire the business to his children. He and his wife of more than 50 years, Jestine, had three children. The twins, Julian and Julia, both forty years old and as snobby as they come and Noah, their thirty-five-year-old son, still sowing his wild oats.

Julian had decided early on that he was too good to be a fisherman, the very thought of spending his days smelling pluff mud and trawling shrimp nets was demeaning in his opinion. By his senior year in college he had chosen law school and had become a big time lawyer up north, rarely coming home to South Carolina.

Julia, refined and perfectly southern as a young woman, had done little since her college days and spent most of her time watching soap operas as religiously as others watch the stock market and gossiping with the locals. She had married one of Kirkland's captains, Tucker Donovan. Tucker was a bastard of man, big and burly; he drank too much and carried the weight of the Litchfield name like a crowned jewel. He knew his good fortune when he won over the heart of Julia Litchfield; one day it would all be his.

Noah had finished college and chosen to return home to work for his father. He knew the business as well as Kirkland and had made his father a lot of money. To Kirkland, Noah was a godsend when it came to Litchfield Shrimp, but from a father's perspective, Noah had a world of growing up to do. Fast cars, wild women, bar hopping, and a carefree attitude that all was good with the world as long as you had a new girl on the horizon or a new car to buy. The elder Litchfields worried that Noah would never find a good girl, settle down and make a name for himself.

Kirkland and Jestine had given the children everything they could have ever wanted, taught them that hard work provided those luxuries, brought them up in church and instilled in them a strong respect for God and family. Regardless, each of the three children had taken paths their parents regretted. Retirement was the dream that Kirkland and Jestine worked for and dreamed of for countless years, but they had no notion of how or to whom, they would put in charge of Litchfield Shrimp.

****

Noah smiled as he walked back down to the boats. *Not bad, not bad at all*, he thought to himself. The friend, Moby, was pretty good. Red hair, cute little-freckled nose, nice big tits. The doctor though, she's the one that really got his testosterone flowing. Blonde hair halfway down her back, eyes as green as the Atlantic and a contagious smile with teeth that had probably never seen a cavity. Oh yeah, his juices were flowing all right; had made his welcoming appearance and left them fighting over him. Jasper and Sumpter Antley were hosing down the 'Miss Claire Anne' when Noah jumped aboard.

"Man, ya look lak ya jis seen a angel!" Sumpter called out to him.

"Yeah," Jasper broke in, smiling at Noah, "but dere ain't no angels on dat dere mind, he got da debil in his head!"

"Jasper, that's one beautiful woman moving in that house up there . . ." Noah said, motioning up the hill. Jasper just shook his head.

"Her pretty, huh, Noah?" Sumpter asked, wanting to hear more.

"Sumpter, that doc's got legs so long, I'd bet this year's profits she could wrap them around me twice!" Noah laughed.

"Galdamity, Noah! Yo pa hare ya yakking like dat, he gonna yank yo tongue right outcha mouth!" Jasper scolded him.

Noah just laughed and patted Jasper on the

back. "Oh, Jasp, I believe I'm going to have to see if the good Dr. Blaylock makes house calls."

****

Madison Blaylock was reluctant to take the new job. She was thirty three years old, single and scared of moving to a new town by herself, especially such a small town like Canton Cope. Her parents had died, together, in an auto accident three years earlier and being their only child, she was left with only a scattering of cousins.

Moving to the Cope meant leaving her friends behind and making a whole new life for herself. The thought of not being able to visit her parents' grave sites as often as she wanted, saddened her greatly. Although she could not see them, hug them or hear them, she knew her mom and dad could hear her and she could still feel their presence with her. Maddie knew this was a decision her parents would have encouraged her to make. *"Spread your wings, Maddie . . . ,"* she could almost hear her mother say.

All and all, the job offer had been too good to pass up. Canton Cope needed a full-time doctor after their resident physician retired after serving 50 plus years to the town. Besides offering a handsome salary, the town's small council administration had included the offer of an adorable house at a really great price.

The house, which was more of a cottage, overlooked the bay and had a beautiful view of the harbor, which was home to the fleets of Litchfield Shrimp. It needed some work, maybe a little bit of a woman's touch, but basically ready to move in to. Maddie had hired a contractor to paint the house, inside and out, and refinish the hardwood floors. In the weeks before the final move, she and her best friend since high school, Moby Muller, had made the two hours' drive to the Cope to hang wallpaper, shelf-paper cabinets and weed out long forgotten flower beds.

By the time moving day arrived, the house was ready for Maddie. She and Moby had their cars filled to the brim with boxes, as well as a packed full U-haul trailer. They spent nearly two days unloading, arranging and rearranging Maddie's things until they had it 'just right'.

"I don't even know why I'm bothering to hang these pictures," Moby sighed. "I know when I leave here, you're gonna hang 'em somewhere else anyway."

"Well, you know me," Maddie laughed, "I'll live with it like it is for a while until I decide I like 'em better somewhere else."

"Exactly! And that's when you better not *even* call me back up here to tell you if this picture's cattywompus!" Moby joked.

Maddie and Moby threw together a Caesar salad and opened a bottle of wine for supper. They ate out on the deck overlooking the bay, laughing and giggling like teenagers, talking about their encounter with Noah Litchfield. As they spoke of the devil himself, Moby caught sight of him leaving the harbor.

"Mmmm, look," she said with a mouthful of lettuce. Maddie looked up just in time to see Noah climbing into his black Jeep Wrangler. As he pulled through the gate, he glanced up the hill, and waved at them with a big grin. The ladies both smiled and waved back.

"Well, you were right about one thing. I'm going to have to do some detective work," Maddie said.

****

Early Monday morning Maddie left for her

office to start her first day. Her staff consisted of her receptionist Caroline Perrin, a lifelong resident of the Cope, and one nurse, a Jamaican born implant to the Cope, Alline Wynn. Caroline reminded Maddie of Mayberry's Aunt Bee, only younger and Alline was Mother Love incarnate, only with attitude. They both welcomed Maddie with open arms and Maddie was sure she had made the right decision to move to the Cope.

Some eight hours later, after seeing a handful of patients, she climbed into her Civic and headed home. It was exactly 5:15 and she was finished for the day. Being in a small town might not be so bad after all. She changed into a pair of shorts and running shoes, pulled her hair into a pony tail and went for a little jog around town.

The warm spring afternoon air filled her lungs, relaxed her, cleared her mind and gave her time to close the door on her work day. Besides, it was a good way to see some of the town as well.

The community was exceptionally beautiful. The town square was cobblestoned with park benches and flower beds here and there. In the middle was a bronze statue of some Civil War soldier or town founder, Maddie wasn't sure, she didn't stop to read the plaque. She made a mental note to come back later and read it, along with a few other historical markers throughout the square.

The houses were vintage seaside homes, with lawns meticulously kept. Fishing boats in nearly every yard, rockers on every porch, American and South Carolina flags flying from banisters, typical ocean living, Anytown, USA.

On the edge of town sat the Litchfield home. As Maddie had expected, it was a turn of the century, massive southern home. The house was at least a hundred years old, three stories tall, white clapboard siding, wraparound porches on each floor, a beautiful lawn, all enclosed with what looked like a custom made wrought iron fence. Just high enough to make a statement, but obviously not meant to keep anyone out, it was simply for aesthetic purposes. Inside the fence, toward the back of the house, Maddie saw a breathtaking garden. The Litchfields obviously had a gardener year round as this garden looked like it was well maintained. It reminded her of the gardens of the homes on the Battery back in Charleston. It made her a little homesick. *'Some people . . . ,'* she thought, *'just have to show it off.'*

As she rounded the bay and headed down by the harbor, Maddie saw Noah securing one of the boats to the dock. "Hi, Noah!" she called out as she jogged by. Noah looked up and saw her run by. "*Sweet mother of god, those legs*," he whispered to himself as he waved back. He dropped the rope and broke into a jog. Within seconds he was running alongside Maddie.

"Hi," he said as he reached her side.

"Hey, Noah," Maddie grinned, looking up at him.

"You do this every day?"

"Every day that I can. How 'bout you?"

"Only when I see a gorgeous doctor go by," Noah grinned back, flirting. Maddie started up the hill with Noah struggling to keep up. She reached her back yard and watched him as he made his way behind her.

"Jesus, doc!" Noah panted. "You training for the Olympics?" Maddie smiled and brushed a stray hair back from her face.

"Noah, what exactly can I do for you?" She was a little curious and a little miffed that he had followed her home.

"Hmmm, doc, is that a proposition?"

"No!" she replied emphatically. "I was thinking more on the line of something to drink before you pass out on me."

"Yeah, yeah, sure. That's what I meant, too. Some lemonade or water would be great."

"I thought so," Maddie smirked. "Have a seat. I'll be right back." Maddie went inside to fetch some lemonade and Noah collapsed in an Adirondack chair. She returned with two glasses of ice and a pitcher of cold lemonade.

"Thanks, doc," Noah said as Maddie handed him a glass.

"You know you can call me Maddie."

"Ahhh, not too keen on the nickname, huh?"

"No, I just get this picture of Doc from Gunsmoke, or Bugs Bunny when I hear 'doc', I'm kind of funny that way."

"Well, let me let you in on a little secret there, 'doc'. I never saw anything as fine as you on Gunsmoke and I sure as hell don't think of little rabbits when I call you 'doc'.

Maddie blushed. "Thank you. Now tell me, do you always follow women home?"

"Like I said, only the gorgeous ones."

"I take it your wife doesn't know you flirt like this with all the pretty girls, does she?"

"Wife??" Noah choked on his drink. "I'm not married! What in god's name made you think I was married?"

"I...I just assumed."

"Well, you assumed wrong. I am *very* single. Haven't found a woman yet that'll live with me."

"That says a lot about you, now doesn't it?" Maddie poked a little fun.

"Yeah, I guess it does."

"So you mean to tell me you live in that big house all by yourself?"

"No, my parents live in that big house. I live across town actually, right off Shad Creek."

"Oh, so are you an only child? Any brothers or sisters?" Maddie asked.

"Damn, I wish. I've got an older brother and sister, twins actually. Julian and Julia."

"Don't say that, you're lucky. I'm an only child."

"I'd have to disagree with you there, Maddie. You are the lucky one. Julian's a big wig lawyer in D.C. and Julia sits on her can all day talking about everybody else." Noah sighed, a heavy breath that let Maddie know he was not at all in good standing with his siblings.

"Noah, that's not very nice to say . . . I mean I realize that all families have their little quirks, but I'd give anything to have a brother or sister."

"You'd have to know them, is the only thing I can tell you, Maddie. Julian never comes home and Julia's jerk of a husband works for my father and thinks he owns the place."

"I'm sorry, Noah. I can't imagine it's all that bad, though."

"Don't be sorry. It's a situation that I have no control over and I just take it as it comes. I have as little contact with them as possible and that seems to keep the peace, so to speak," Noah paused for a second, trying to find a way to change the subject. "Look, I don't want to talk about Julian and Julia. Let me ask you something . . ." Maddie smiled, welcoming a change of atmosphere.

Noah took a deep breath and asked, "I was wondering if you'd like to have dinner with me one night? Let me show you the town . . ."

Maddie took a moment to think about Noah's question, and shook her head, smiling slightly. "I don't think so, Noah. Not right now. I'm new here, and there's so much I need to do to get established in the community. It's not that I wouldn't love to, but right now I think I need to focus on my job. I don't need any distractions . . . just yet," she smiled at Noah, hoping he understood.

Noah wasn't used to rejections, especially from women. But he hid his disappointment well. "I understand that, completely. Let's keep the invitation open, though?"

"Absolutely," Maddie agreed.

Noah finished his glass of lemonade, said

goodbye and headed back to the docks. Sumpter was grinning like a Cheshire cat when Noah returned.

"Okay, Noah, where's ya takin' her?" he asked excitedly.

"Nowhere, Sumpter, that woman just turned me down!" Noah answered a little angrily.

"Her don't sound too crazy da me," Sumpter chuckled, "sound like hers got some smarts!"

"Don't be so sure of yourself, man. She'll come around; I've just got to give her some time. She will come around." Noah was certain of that.

****

Moby called the next night to see how Maddie was doing and to tell her how much she and everyone back home missed her. They talked about their jobs and Moby filled Maddie in on all the gossip and goings-on back home. Moby was a high school guidance counselor and once again, was having her share of problematic students. But those kids had one good thing going for them. . . Moby Muller. If there ever was a more dedicated, sympathetic, but stubborn as hell, guidance counselor, Maddie had never met one. Moby went above and beyond for 'her kids', as she called them.

"So . . . ," Moby asked slyly, "have you seen that hunk, Noah Litchfield, again?"

Maddie laughed, "Funny you should ask. He actually asked me out last night."

"He what?" Moby screamed, obviously thrilled.

"I went running after work, he saw me, caught up with me and asked me out. That's it."

"Oh . . . my . . . god! That's great! Oh, lord, that man is so fine . . . where's he taking you?"

"Nowhere, I'm not going out with him."

"What?" Moby gasped. "Are you crazy? The man is gorgeous and R - I - C - H. . . . What is wrong with you?"

"Moby, he's thirty-five, has never been married, I've seen him around town with ALL kinds of women. I don't want to be a name on his list, you know?"

"Then give him my number! Gawd, did your moma drop you on your head when you were born or what??" Moby groaned.

"No, she did not," Maddie grinned into the phone, "but whose mother named *her* after some fictitious albino whale??"

"Hey, it was the sixties, okay? She was married to my *Dad* for Pete's sake, give the woman a break. And screw your head back on and go out with Noah!”

CHAPTER TWO

Several weeks later, Maddie was getting the hang of things and making friends fast in Canton Cope. The locals were warming up to her and she finally felt like she was settling in. As she sat on the sofa late one evening, going over some patients' charts, a loud rap at the door startled her. She went to the door and looking out the window, saw Noah clutching a bloody rag to his hand. There was a short, black man with him. She swung the door open.

"Noah, what happened? Come in!"

"Sliced my hand with an oyster knife," he confessed.

"Sit down and let me get a look at it." Maddie motioned for him to sit on a kitchen stool and removed the rag, as blood gushed from the open wound. She wiped the gash clean with sterile gauze and pulled back the folds of skin to see how deep the cut was.

"Owh!" Noah groaned.

"Sorry, I know it hurts."

"How bad is it?" he asked.

"It's pretty deep. You're going to need some stitches. Have you got your car?"

"It's down at the docks."

Maddie nodded, "That's okay. I'll drive you myself. We need to go to the office and get this stitched closed."

"Noah, ya needs me to go wif ya?" The older man looked concerned.

"Nah, Jasp, you go on home. Thanks for getting me up here," Noah replied. The man nodded at Noah and tipped his hat to Maddie as he walked out the door.

"Who's your friend?" Maddie asked, wrapping Noah's hand with clean gauze.

"That's Jasper Hampton. He's worked for us his whole life. They don't come any better than Jasper."

"It was nice of him to make sure you got here."

"He's like a brother to me. Hell, he treats me better than my own brother."

"Let's go," Maddie said, taking Noah's arm.

****

Maddie unlocked the office door and flipped on the lights. The fluorescent lights flickered and came to life. "Go right in there, Noah and I'll get some Novocain." She returned with two syringes of clear liquid and went right to work on numbing Noah's hand. Beads of sweat broke out on his forehead as Maddie probed the needle inside his hand. He didn't think she'd ever get through sticking him with that needle.

"I know this isn't pleasant, but you don't want to feel anything, do you?" Maddie asked when she noticed Noah flinching. Noah just shook his head 'no' as he felt a wave of nausea fall over him. *'Damn, I don't need to look like a pussy to this woman, get it together Noah,'* he thought as she continued to look at his hand.

"So how did this happen?" Maddie asked, as she waited for the Novocain to start its wonderful sleeping job.

"Shucking oysters. The knife just slipped."

"You know, most people wear a glove when they're shucking oysters, Noah."

"Ha, ha, very funny. I know that, but gloves just get in my way."

"Hmmmmm, I can see the alternative is much better." Maddie smiled at him, trying to get him to relax. She worked on his hand for over an hour, taking almost 17 stitches to close the gaping wound. She finished off by giving him a tetanus shot, just in case.

"I want you to keep this hand dry until the stitches come out. Wash around it, wear a baggie in the shower, or take a bath instead, whatever, just don't get it wet."

"Well, now Maddie, if push comes to shove, you could give me a bath tonight," Noah joked.

"Noah! I'm being serious."

"Well, so was I. Can't blame a man for trying."

Sweet Dreams, Doc

Maddie drove Noah back to the harbor and to his car. "If you need anything for pain, take a couple of ibuprofen every four or five hours. Remember to keep it dry and I want to see you in a week. If it hurts more than you think it should, come to the office and I'll check to make sure it isn't infected."

"So, you want to see me in a week, huh? What did you have in mind?" Noah asked playfully.

"At my office, wise ass. To remove the stitches." She smiled back at him.

"You know, Maddie, I've never done it in a doctor's office before . . ." He gave her another one of those million dollar smiles.

"Good night, Noah," Maddie laughed as she pushed him out of her car.

"Thanks for being there tonight." Noah stepped from her car. "Sweet dreams, doc."

Noah left Maddie feeling flushed and surprisingly aroused. He had a way about him that made her know he was a great lover and she couldn't help but imagine what it would be like to be in his arms. On the other hand, Noah had quite the reputation around town as a rambler. She saw how he flirted and carried on with every woman he came in contact with, married or not. Maddie didn't need that in her life, no way, no how.

She came home from work the following evening to find a cluster of fresh wild flowers on her back steps, lying next to a bottle of wine. Attached to the wine bottle was a card. *"Guess it's official now . . . I get to call you 'doc'. Thanks for taking care of me! Noah."* Maddie smiled and looked down at the harbor; sure enough, there was Noah standing out there watching her. She smiled and waved at him as he waved back with his bandaged hand. *'Oh yeah, Mr. Litchfield,'* she thought to herself, *'you are one smooth operator.'* Noah watched Maddie as she picked up the bottle of wine and read the note. *'Won't be long, doc, won't be long and I'm going to have you eating out of my hand, stitches and all.'*

****

One week later, and not a minute beyond, Noah was at Maddie's office first thing that morning. He walked right past Caroline and headed to Maddie's private office. He quietly tapped on her door. "Morning, doc," he smiled.

"Hey there. Let's get a look at that hand." Maddie gently removed the bandage and examined his hand. "Looks like they're ready to come out. It's healed up nicely, Noah."

"Well, you did a great job with that needle and thread yourself, you know," he praised her, although she knew he was just dangling more bait.

"Okay, Alline's going to take them out, but I want you to wear this brace," she handed him a box with some sort of stretch brace in it. "Wear it for about two weeks to make sure the muscle has healed properly, too."

Noah moaned, "Oh, Maddie, don't send that battle ax in here. I like your hands much better."

"Sorry, Noah," she laughed, "I have other patients to see. Now be a good boy and I'll make sure Caroline gives you a lolly pop." She left Noah sulking as she walked out the room. '*Dammit,*" Noah cursed to himself, *'what is her problem?'* Alline came in to find Noah all but pouting.

"What be yo problem, mon? Yer scered?" Alline snickered.

"Don't be stupid, Alline. What's the deal with Dr. Blaylock?"

"Problem? Like what?" Alline quizzed.

"Is she a lesbian? Is that the answer? I mean, if she is, that's great. That's super, that would explain a lot. But is she?" Noah was as dumbfounded as a redneck in a spelling bee.

"Noah Litchfield! Boy, I bet I'll slap yo mouth, ya keep talkin' like that!" she scolded him.

"Hell, Alline! I've done everything to impress that woman, flowers, wine, the great smile, southern charm . . . I mean I've been laying it on thick. She won't even look twice at me!"

"Well, now Noah, yer gonna be mad at me, mon, but with yer track record, ya could make any woman wanna be a girl lovah."

"That isn't funny, Alline. Am I that bad of a guy?"

"Baby, let me 'xplain somin' to ya. You a sweet boy, got a lot to offer anybody. But ya parade all over da town like a playboy all de time. You 'spect somebody like Maddie to want to be one of 'dem kinda girls? Come on now, boy, ya smarta dan dat!"

"So what are you saying, Alline? I'm supposed to change my entire lifestyle to get a date with one woman?" Noah was perplexed.

"Depends on da woman, how bad ya want her and what kinda relationship you be wantin' wid her. Now you sits back and thank 'bout dat fer a while, eh?"

When Alline finished removing his stitches, he collected his candy sucker from Caroline, paid his bill and turned to leave the office when Caroline stopped him. "Oh, Noah, Dr. Blaylock wanted me to be sure and give you these," she handed him a bag from the hardware store. "She said to be sure and use these next time." Caroline was grinning big time. Noah reached in the bag and pulled out a new pair of Wells LaMont working gloves. Everyone knows they're the best shucking gloves ever made and not one man with a love of the sea had less than three or four pairs at all times.

Noah smirked and sucked on his teeth, "Oh, now she's just being a smart ass...." *'That's it'*, he decided on the ride back to the harbor, *'weeks of trying, all in vain. Time to move on. There's plenty of women on this peninsula that I won't have to change for.'* Noah didn't like rejection, but there was a first time for everything.

CHAPTER THREE

Maddie spent the weekend back home, in Charleston, tying up all the loose ends in the sale of her parents home. She had kept the remaining land for future investments or maybe even to build her own home on one day. Charleston would always be home and she couldn't imagine raising a family anywhere else in the world. Moby wanted to be with her, but Maddie wanted to do this alone. She had goodbyes to say and memories to lock away. After one last walk through the house and taking even more pictures for keepsakes, she drove out to the cemetery to tell her parents it was done and that she hoped she had done the right thing. Somehow she knew her parents would be pleased, proud and would approve of her selling the house. *'Spread your wings, Maddie . . .'* She could almost hear her mom whispering in her ear as she placed flowers on their graves.

Sweet Dreams, Doc

****

The first of May brought the beginning of shrimp season to the Cope and the town was all abuzz about the upcoming Blessing of the Fleet. Maddie had never been to the one in Mt. Pleasant before, but found herself excited about this one. She was anxious to see what all the fuss was about and to be a part of the historical annual event. There were dozens of food booths, art displays, and a carnival for the children and a live band playing on the harbor. At exactly noon, the priest of *Our Mother Mary Catholic Church of Canton Cope* motioned for the music to stop as he took the microphone.

The trawlers had all been whitewashed and were gleaming in the afternoon sun, all docked side by side at the marina. Each captain and his crew were aboard their own boats and Maddie noticed Noah right away with an older gentleman that had to be his father. They were standing on the landing with the priest as he began the annual blessing.

"Good people of Canton Cope, welcome! We are gathered here today, in this beautiful place - God's glory all around us - as we commence to wish our blessings on this year's shrimping season. Today we gather to bless these ships and these boats, those who work on them; those who provide food from these waters and those who use these waters for family and pleasure. Let us pray." The priest bowed his head and the spectators followed suit.

"Our Father, we ask your presence upon this event of the blessing of the fleet. We thank you for the beauty of the earth and the mighty waters that surround the land. May we be responsible for the just and proper use of your creation. Like the psalmist of old, we cry unto you for the protections of those who go down to the sea in ships. In your holy name, we pray. Amen."

"Amen," Maddie replied.

The man standing next to Noah stepped up to the mike and opened a Bible. He began reading the Sailor's Psalm, Psalm 107, verses 23 through 31:

"Others went out to sea in ships; they werc merchants on the mighty waters. They saw the works of the Lord, his wonderful deeds in the deep. For he spoke and stirred up a tempest that lifted high the waves. They mounted up to the heavens and went down to the depths; in their peril their courage melted away. They reeled and staggered like drunken men; they were at their wits' end. Then they cried out to the Lord in their trouble, and He brought them out of their distress. He stilled the storm to a whisper; the waves of the sea were hushed. They were glad when it grew calm, and He guided them to their desired haven. Let them give thanks to the Lord for His unfailing love and His wonderful deeds for men. Let them exalt Him in the assembly of the people and praise Him in the council of the elders."

His voice resounded through the harbor and he needed no microphone. Maddie thought he spoke so eloquently and so soulfully. She wasn't sure who he was, but as Alline stepped up beside her, she whispered to Maddie, "That be Noah's father, Kirkland Litchfield. He a fine mon." The music started again and the crowd began singing the first strains of the National Anthem. When the music came to a quiet hush, the trawlers began their journey past the wharf, chugging along slowly. The priest uncovered a vat of holy water and with an olive branch, dipped into the water and touched the branch to each trawler as it made its way past him. As he touched each boat, he made the sign of the cross. Maddie was sorry now she had never gone to Mt. Pleasant to witness the blessing there because she found it to be very moving. She'd never realized how meaningful the event was and how seriously these people took this endeavor of making a living on the sea.

Noah was watching Maddie and hoped no one noticed. He'd participated in the blessing of the fleet all his life and it wasn't that he found it boring or trite, just the opposite. Noah took to heart every word of every prayer, scripture and song. His father had instilled in him many years ago that these men and their hard work were the livelihood of Litchfield Shrimp and it was Litchfield's responsibility to keep them safe. But for the life of him, he couldn't stop glancing at Maddie. She seemed so entranced by the whole thing and listening intently to every word. Noah was guessing she'd never been to a fleet blessing before.

When the last trawler was blessed and all headed out to sea, the priest asked the crowd to one last time bow their heads and pray with him.

"God of boundless love, at the beginning of creation your spirit hovered over the deep. You called forth every creature and the seas teamed with life. Your son Jesus calmed the Sea of Galilee, brought His disciplines to safety, and filled their nets. He has given us the rich harvest of salvation. Bless these boats, the equipment and all who serve on them and who would use them. Protect them from the dangers of wind and rain and of the perils of the deep. Bring us all to the harbor of light and peace. May the saving power of our Lord, guide and protect us all. In the name of God the Father, the Son and the Holy Spirit. Amen."

When the last of the ceremony was over, Noah stepped down from the platform and made his way through the crowd to reach Maddie. She was already enjoying a corn dog the size of an ear of corn and sucking on a huge cup of Coke. He touched her arm to get her attention.

"Afternoon, doc. Enjoy the blessing?" He smiled.

"Actually, I did, Noah, it was something else. I've never been before and it was really touching. How have you been?" She smiled back.

"Busy as usual. Working, playing, whatever passes the time." Noah flirted.

"Yep, that's exactly what I thought,"

Maddie smirked.

"What does that mean?" Noah frowned.

"Just that....whatever or *whoever* passes the time. Isn't that more like it?" She took a big bite of the corn dog and washed it down with a big gulp of Coke. She had insulted Noah instantly and he turned red; immediately she was sorry for saying it. His personal life was none of her business and she really could have cared less how he spent his time or with whom.

"Doc, now you wouldn't be a tad jealous, would you?" Noah tried to play off his hurt feelings.

"Ha," Maddie chuckled, "hardly. Have a great afternoon Noah." With that, she turned from him and walked off in the direction of her house.

Noah just shook his head and mumbled under his breath, *"bitch"*.

CHAPTER FOUR

Maddie had been in Canton Cope for several months now and was feeling like it was home. The townspeople had brought her gifts of food or books on the local history; some brought canned tomatoes or beans, baskets of fresh vegetables and of course, always, fresh shrimp. She started attending services at the Baptist church in the square and finally began to feel comfortable, even happy.

Maddie saw Noah around town several times, more times than not, he'd have a woman with him. It seemed he had no particular taste in women, other than large breasts and long legs. As to their intelligence or social status, Maddie couldn't decide, but they clung to him like he was a prize they had won at the county fair, therefore she summed up their IQ on that little fact. His ego was as big as the Atlantic and apparently so was his libido.

Noah hadn't quite given up on Maddie, though, calling every so often, asking her to this function or that function. She was polite, but continued to decline all of his invitations. Noah Litchfield obviously had one thing in mind: score big with the doctor and add another notch in his belt. Maddie had no plans of being a number or a notch for Mr. Litchfield.

****

Late one afternoon, Jasper Hampton paid her a visit at the office. As he sat down in the exam room, Maddie noticed he looked nervous, almost frightened.

"Jasper, what's the problem this morning?"

"Doc Blaylock, I ain't sick."

"Okay, then. What can I do for you?" Maddie was now curious.

"Well, I jis wanna talk atcha 'bout somein'," Jasper was all but shaking.

"That's fine, Jasper. That's what I'm here for. You can talk to me about anything," she gently patted his big, calloused hand. He was a fine man and she knew he was greatly troubled or he wouldn't be in front of her now.

"Even Noah?" Jasper cautiously asked, looking down at his feet.

"Well," she hesitated, "of course. If Noah has a problem, or is in trouble, it's very nice of you to be concerned. How can I help you, help Noah?"

"Doc, I mighty troubled 'bout dat boy."

"Go ahead, Jasper."

"Is troublin' him bad dat ya ain't got nuttin' to do wid him," Jasper confessed.

"Jasper!" Maddie couldn't believe her ears. "I have ailing patients waiting to see me and you come in here with this nonsense. He put you up to this, didn't he? Tell me!"

"No, no, Miss Maddie, let me talk now. My nerves be messin' wid me for a long time now over dis. I knowed dat boy all his life and I's tellin' ya, he be bad off. Now I know he ain't whatcha lookin' for in no man, hell, he ain't what no *decent* gal be lookin' for, but he a good boy and he be in bad shape right now." Jasper apparently had thought this through and as nervous as he looked, Maddie could only assume Noah hadn't sent him after all.

"Jasper, why on earth is this so important to you, to him? Why is he so hell bent on getting me to go on a date with him?" Maddie was totally confused and frustrated. "Is his little black book that important to him, he's just got to get a doctor in that book? What?"

"Miss Maddie, Doc Blaylock, Noah always been wild and takin' up wid ever gal he could git his hands on. But he jis been runnin', runnin' from ever thing that meant growin' up, being a man. But he done got you in hissin' head and he ain't been wid no gal in weeks," Jasper was talking ninety miles a minute now and Maddie was shaking her head.

"No, no, no . . . that's not true Jasper. Now I've seen Noah with several ladies, and I use that term loosely, in the past few weeks and he seems just fine."

"He been doing dat ta eat atcha. He figurin' ya'd git green and change yo mind."

"My goodness, he is full of himself. I can assure you I am not jealous and I can't believe that Noah would think seeing him with other women would make me want to go out with him. He's got some nerve," now Maddie was taking ninety miles a minute.

"Doc, ya is jis what dat boy be needin'. Ya is da firs gal I ever seen him want so bad dat was decent. And das why he be wantin' ya so bad . . . you's a good lady, and he be knowd dat. You could git dat boy to settle down some and I thinks dat's why he wants ya in a bad way. He don't want no note in dat book he got...it ain't 'bout dat. He be knowin' ya could scraightun him up and in his head, he be wantin' dat. Ya jis gotta give him a chance, dat's all I's axin'. Please...." Jasper was as sincere as he could be and Maddie couldn't help but remember the night Noah cut his hand. He'd told her Jasper was like a brother to him, better than his own brother. She stood up and led Jasper to the door, "Tell Caroline there's no charge for your visit and I'll think about what you said."

"Please don' tell Noah I had been here. He'd be mighty ticked off wid me," Jasper pleaded with Maddie.

"This conversation never happened, Jasper." Maddie plopped down in the chair when Jasper was gone. Could it be that Noah didn't send Jasper to talk to her? Was it possible that he was just trying to make her jealous? Was he really a much better man than she'd thought? *"no way, Blaylock, he's not a better man than you think he is..."* she thought to herself.

Sweet Dreams, Doc

CHAPTER FIVE

A couple of weeks after her surprise visit from Jasper Hampton, Maddie found herself sitting on the deck looking at the stars and thinking of her parents, her visit with Jasper and how she wished her mom were here for her to talk to about it all.

The trawlers were making their way back into the harbor and as night had caught them, they turned on their running lights. A few had strings of white lights along their casting poles and Maddie couldn't help but think about the Christmas boat parade in Charleston.

Every year, anyone with a boat of any kind, yacht, schooner, canoe, tugboat, sailboat, it didn't matter as long as it could float, would decorate their vessels in Christmas fashion. As soon as the sun set and the moon was high in the sky, those boats would parade through Charleston Harbor and the Waterfront Park. Literally hundreds of spectators would gather to watch the parade of lights as they quietly drifted by. It was a beautiful sight to see, and seeing the trawlers now, made Maddie extremely homesick. She made a silent vow to make the drive to Charleston this year to see the parade.

Just then she glimpsed someone coming up the hill to her back yard and was startled. It was too late for company and she was alone. Only when the figure emerged from the shadows and triggered the motion sensor floodlight, did she relax. It was Noah.

"Hi, Doc," he sounded down.

"Do you often walk into people's yards after dark?"

"I'm sorry if I scared you, Maddie. I saw you sitting up here and was wondering if we could talk." Maddie thought about Jasper, what he'd want, and decided it couldn't hurt to just talk to Noah.

"Sure, sit down. Are you okay?"

"My father's retiring."

"Well, Noah, that's wonderful, don't you think? He's worked hard for a long time, and I think it's past time for him and your mom to enjoy life."

"I know he has. Litchfield wouldn't be what it is today without him. He has every right to walk away now and travel the world, which is what he and Mother have always wanted to do. I'm just afraid if he walks away now, dependent on his decisions as to who he turns the business over to, it won't ever be the same again," Noah explained, almost mournful. “He hasn’t discussed with me which of the three of us he plans on putting in charge.”

Maddie hesitated before answering, “Noah, I think you’re being selfish.” She was regretting what she said the minute she said it. But Noah didn’t react in the way she expected.

“No, no I’m not being selfish. Julian could care less about the business. He’s made his own fortune, so he’d only turn around and sell it out from under me. And Julia would only want to turn it over to Tucker. That bastard would lose it within the first year.”

“So I’m guessing you think you should left in charge?”

“Maddie, I know this business like the back of my hand. I’ve worked for, and with my father since I was eight. As soon as I was old enough to cast a net, I was on a trawler. Even when I was in college, every summer I was back on those docks. I know Dad isn't too proud of my lifestyle, but it never interfered with Litchfield. He taught me everything he learned from his father and I've always done it his way. With the introduction of computers and better technology, Dad always had a tried and true way to dredge those lines and I never doubted him. He said we didn't need fancy machines and he was right. I just can't imagine what would happen if Julian or Tucker got their hands on it."

"It sounds like your father has a big decision to make and he'll do what is best for Litchfield. You have to trust him now just like you have always. And Noah," Maddie continued, "if it means turning it over to your brother or sister, you'll just have to accept it. Don't let his decision affect your relationship with your father. You'll regret it when he's gone. I know."

"Has your father passed away, Doc?" Noah didn't think he knew that.

"Yep. My mom, too. They were killed in a car accident three years ago. Truck driver went to sleep, crossed the center line."

"Maddie, I'm so sorry, I had no idea. It must have been so hard losing them both at the same time. . . and being an only child."

"My father and I were never very close, we loved each other, but we never really told each other. And it's extremely hard now, wishing he were here so I could tell him. Whatever happens, Noah, let your father know you love him and respect his decision, no matter what he decides."

Noah reached over and squeezed Maddie's hand. "Thank you, Maddie. I needed this. I needed someone to tell me what was important."

"Don't worry," she smiled at Noah, "you'll

get a bill."

As Noah stood to leave, he gently pulled Maddie to him. "Forgive me, Doc," he whispered as he bent to kiss her. It was a tender kiss that left Maddie completely defenseless. He brushed her hair back from her face and said so softly she almost didn't hear him, "I've wanted to do that for a long time."

"Noah, I don't know what to say."

"Don't say anything. I'm not going to ask to stay and I'm not going to put your name in my infamous black book. I just want a chance. I want a chance to do something right for a change. Just give me some time, give us some time."

Before Maddie could force any words from her mouth, Noah kissed her again. Just as softly as the first time, sweetly and purely perfect. "Sweet dreams, Doc," he whispered in her ear as he turned to leave. Maddie stood there in the dark and watched him make his way to the harbor. Even then she couldn't think of a thing she would have said to him if she could have made herself talk.

CHAPTER SIX

Knock! Knock! Knock, knock! Maddie pried her eyes open thinking she must have been dreaming, but then it came again. A loud rap on her front door. *'Good lord, it's Saturday morning, who in the world...'* she mumbled as she crawled from her bed. She opened the door to find Noah standing in her doorway.

"Noah, what are you doing here? It's five a.m. . . . and Saturday!!"

"Get on some jeans and a t-shirt. You're going with me today." Noah declared.

"I am? And where might that be?" Maddie frowned, hands on her hips.

"On the boat. Get a move on, Doc, time's a wasting. And bring a jacket, it gets a little chilly on the water after dark."

Maddie shook her head. "What if I have other plans? You can't just breeze in here and assume I'm going to drop everything and go with you."

"Maddie, I want you to go with me. So are you going or not?"

She stood there, just staring at him, thinking she knew she needed to stay away from him. But he was making it almost impossible. *'Oh, god, I know I'm going to regret this'*, she thought to herself. "Give me a minute to put on some clothes. Come on in." She returned ten minutes later, dressed as requested, jeans and a tee, with a jacket in tow, hair pulled through a baseball cap. No make-up, but brushed teeth.

"What if there's an emergency? What if I'm needed back here?" she asked.

"Jasper knows you'll be with me. He'll reach us on the radio if you're needed."

"How were you so sure I'd go with you?"

Noah just smiled, "I wasn't. I just really hoped you would."

The day was beautiful and the water calm. Maddie expected it to be more rough since they were so far out, but amazingly the seas were calm. She watched with true interest as Noah and Sumpter worked the dredge lines and pulled in net after net of shrimp.

Although she found the whole experience exciting, she really enjoyed finding the treasures the nets brought up along with the shellfish. Most of the treasures were indeed just trash, but she did find some beautiful shells and a New York license plate. The license plate was dated 1966, which was the year she was born. Taking that as a sign that she was meant to be on that trawler today, she kept it.

Maddie thought it would make a nice conversation piece and decided to hang it inside her outdoor storage shed. Moby would get a kick out of it. *'A license plate?'* she'd say. *'It's probably some poor gangster got himself some cement shoes and they disposed of the car.'* Maddie could almost hear Moby laughing.

It was just after noon when Noah called out to Sumpter, "You ready for some lunch?"

"Yessa! My belly be doin' flips!" Sumpter called back, smiling.

Noah lowered the anchor and excusing himself, went into the cabin. He returned with a picnic basket and a blanket. Maddie smiled, a little surprised that he had packed a lunch.

"Noah, you packed a picnic lunch?"

"Well, we do eat while we're out here, you

know. Contrary to popular belief, we have on occasion actually paid the help, too," he smiled back at her.

"So. . . you always bring a blanket and a picnic basket, too? Just how close are you and Sumpter?" Maddie jokingly asked.

"Well, now, I have to be honest. I usually only bring the blanket when I'm with Jasp, Sumpter isn't too keen on sharing one with me," Noah replied with a wink. Sumpter was laughing up a storm.

"Tell da truth, Miss Maddie, dis here be da firs' time I seen Noah wid a basset and a shrow blanket. I tink he might be holin' out on me! I's startin' da feels lef' out..." Sumpter gave Noah a hardy pat on the back. "You's startin' da step out on me, Noah?" Noah just laughed at Sumpter and shook his head as he laid out the blanket and began unpacking the contents of the basket.

"Hmmm, shrimp salad? You out did yourself today, Noah." Maddie smiled.

"Yeah, well, you know it was hard getting it all stuffed in these croissants, but I did what I could, " Noah gave her a little smirk. Just as she was starting to believe him, he confessed. "Nah, I can't take credit for this. Jasper's wife, Sadie. . . I don't think you've met her yet. She works over at the Canton Café and she makes the best shrimp salad you'll ever taste. Her chicken salad isn't too bad, either."

Maddie gave Noah a little smile and sipped her iced tea. "Well, I was half expecting peanut butter and jelly sandwiches. This is nice little surprise."

"Truth be told, if lunch had been left up to me, that's exactly what we would've been having."

"I've had a really nice time today, Noah. I'm so glad I came."

"I'm really glad you did, too. It wasn't so bad after all, was it?"

"I've definitely seen a side of you that I like, that's for sure."

"I didn't know there was a side of me you didn't like. . ." he joked.

The three enjoyed their lunch, laughing and getting to know each other. Sumpter was a great comedian and Maddie was even happier that he had come along today. She thoroughly enjoyed getting to know him better. As well, spending time with Noah in his world, was a nice change. Maddie had to admit that after watching him for the last few hours, she had come to certainly appreciate the look of old jeans, a white t-shirt, a baseball cap and flip-flops on a tall, handsome man. Even the black crocs Noah slipped on his feet once aboard the trawler looked good on him.

She helped him gather their lunch leftovers and packed the basket, before putting it back in the cabin. Maddie had an idea, and she wasn't sure if it was a great one, or a careless one, but the moment felt right and she went with it. "So what time are we getting back to the harbor today?" she asked Noah.

"You got plans for tonight or something?" he asked in reply.

"Depends."

"Depends? On what?" Noah's curiosity was peaking.

"Whether or not you say 'yes'."

Noah smiled. He liked where this was going. "What do you have in mind, little lady?"

"Oh, I don't know, I thought I'd take you to dinner tonight. As a way to thank you for today."

"Well, in that case, I guess we'll have to call it an early day, cause I'm saying 'yes'." Noah grinned from ear to ear. "Sumpter!" Noah called out, "how'd you like to get off early today?"

"Dat depend, boss," Sumpter smiled. "You's gonna pay me for da full day?"

"What do you think, wise-ass?" Noah called back.

"I's thinkin' ya gonna pay me, das what I's thinkin'. Ya ain't wont ya ole man be ridin' yo ass, does ya?" Sumpter laughed out loud.

"Ahhh, Sumpter, you know me so well." Noah smiled. "Get on over here and let's get this baby home."

They pulled into the harbor around three

o'clock and after weighing the day's load and icing it down, Sumpter hosed the trawler down while Noah wrote the daily log. Within the hour, he was walking Maddie to her back door. "So what time do you want me to pick you up?" she asked.

Noah shook his head. "No m'am, we're doing this the right way. Can you be ready by seven o'clock?"

Maddie looked at her watch. It was just after four. "Of course, that's nearly three hours. I'm not real high maintenance if you haven't noticed."

"You don't need to be, Doc. I'll see you at seven." He left without attempting to kiss her and she was just ever so slightly disappointed.

"Hey!" Maddie called out to him. "Where are we going?"

"Don't worry about that, Doc. You just be ready at seven."

CHAPTER SEVEN

Maddie showered and stood in her closet, not having a clue what to wear. She had no idea where Noah was taking her and didn't want to end up in some swanky place, dressed like she was going to the Burger Palace. She decided to wear her hair up in a soft twist, a flowing white, cotton sun dress and a pair of white, lace-up espadrille.

The day on the water had given her a sun-kissed glow and the tiny scattered freckles on her nose had decided to make an appearance. She was pacing nervously when Noah arrived, right on the dot, at seven o'clock. He was driving a black BMW convertible and had the top down. *'Geez, he is loaded, that's the second car I've seen him driving since I moved here. I'm still putting around in my 8 year old Civic.'* she thought to herself.

Sweet Dreams, Doc

As he stepped from the car, Maddie forgot all about the BMW and the Jeep Wrangler, even her beat up old Civic. She caught her breath in her throat. *'God, he is so handsome!'* she mumbled as she fidgeted with the door knob. Noah was wearing white linen slacks, a black polo shirt and flip-flops...flip-flops? He was definitely a beach bum. All six feet or better of him was tanned and his sun-bleached chestnut hair was still damp from his recent shower. She noticed it curled just a little bit at the back of his neck. The curl got her. She was hooked. *'Control yourself, Blaylock,'* she whispered to herself as she opened the door.

"Hey, you. Come on in."

Noah took Maddie's hand. "Don't have time, god, you look beautiful! I've made eight o'clock reservations and we need to hustle to make the ferry. Let's go..." he led her out the door and down the walk.

"Ferry?" she asked as he closed her car door.

"Yes, m'am. We're going to Drake Island, ferry leaves in 15 minutes."

"Drake Island. I haven't heard of it before."

They made the ferry just in time. It moved along slowly and the early evening was quiet, give for the seagulls and the frogs. The view was spectacular.

"So where did you make reservations? And how did you make reservations at this late notice?"

"The Veranda. And I know the owner." He smiled.

"The Veranda? Sounds lovely."

"Used to be a big rice plantation in the 17 and 1800's. The family eventually died out, or those left didn't really want the upkeep, so the historical society stepped in and had it turned into a landmark. Some Yankee bought it, paid a hefty price for it, too, and opened the restaurant. That was probably 20 years ago or so."

"Wow, 20 years? The Yankee must be doing pretty good." Maddie laughed.

"Yeah, well, the story doesn't end there."

"Oooo, drama..." Maddie joked.

"And then some. First of all, how's some Yankee going to come down here, open a restaurant in a former rice plantation and serve fine, southern food? He didn't have a clue what collards were, or ham rice, or god forbid, shrimp and grits. And he sure as hell didn't know anything about southern hospitality."

"So how has it done so well all these years?"

"A local man, name of Simon Salley,

propositioned the Yankee into letting him become a partner. I guess the man realized if The Veranda was going to make it, he'd need a real southern influence. And he was right. So right in fact, the south rose again and sent his ass back up north." Noah joked. "Salley bought out the Yankee's half about eleven years ago and never looked back. The place has boomed ever since."

The ferry docked at 7:45 and by 8:00 they were handing the BMW's keys to the valet. Maddie was astounded at the beauty of The Veranda and the landscaping. She felt like she had stepped back in time. Century-old live oaks were scattered throughout the lawns, their ancient limbs practically touching the ground, shading the warm grass. To the left of the restaurant was the Atlantic, it was breathtaking to see as the fading sun reflected on the ocean. Dining was available both inside and out, with tables set up on each of the three wraparound balconies. It was simply put, beautiful.

A young, tuxedo clad man, stood at the door, welcomed them to The Veranda and opened the door for them. Maddie was even more awestruck when she stepped into the restaurant. She could almost see Scarlett standing on the winding staircase, *'Rhett, where shall I go?'* The owner had painstakingly restored the home to its original grandeur and then some. Rich, warm rugs, on mahogany floors, eight inch baseboards, with gorgeous moldings and arches, drapes that probably took five people to hang, beautifully framed oil portraits of the town's founding fathers, mayors, heroes, and ancestors adorned the walls and the antique furniture itself, had to cost a fortune. Maddie felt like a southern belle.

The teenage girl at the hostess table broke into a grin a mile wide when Maddie and Noah walked up. Maddie thought obviously Noah was every school girl's heart throb and she suddenly felt proud to be standing by his side. And then even more suddenly, foolish for feeling proud.

"We have reservations for eight. Litchfield." Noah announced.

"Yes, Mr. Litchfield. Eight o'clock." The girl blushed as she marked Noah's name from the journal on the desk. "We have a quiet table for two ready for you on the Laurel Lanai." She picked up two menus and motioned for them to follow her. She led Noah and Maddie up the wide, winding staircase to the second floor and through huge, French doors onto the expansive porch. They were seated at an elegantly set table, with glasses of water and ice awaiting them. "Your waiter will be with you in a moment. If you need us in the mean time, please just pick up the bell."

"Noah, this has got to be the most beautiful place I've ever been to and having lived in

Charleston all my life, I've seen some beautiful homes. But this place is just beyond any I've ever seen."

"I think it was one of a kind in its day, even now. I'm pretty sure the original family was into more than rice planting. I figure they must have done some bootlegging along the way. . ." Noah smiled. "I thought you'd like it."

"I love it, god, it's so peaceful, too. You know you usually hear the hustle and bustle of people dining and the comings and goings of the employees, but it's so quiet here. I'm just amazed. It's almost like we're in our own home with no interruptions."

"Our own home?" Noah couldn't help but call her on that one.

"Well, you know what I meant."

"Romantic. That's what I think this place

is. I always have."

Maddie blushed a little as she realized what Noah had said, but let it pass by jokingly asking, "So, how many other fine, southern ladies have had the privilege of dining here with you?"

"Actually, Doc," Noah was being honest, "you're the first."

"Right, Noah, right," Maddie snickered.

"Seriously, you are. I've been here with my folks dozens of times. Several times with business clients and even more times for weddings or receptions, but never with a date."

"Why not?"

"Maddie, it's no secret to anyone that the women I've dated aren't exactly the 'Veranda' type. I mean," he shrugged his shoulders, "this isn't exactly the place I'd bring them. Maybe the Cotton

Club, but not here."

Maddie laughed out loud. "Noah! How can you talk about those women that way? After all, you were dating them?"

"Because it's the truth," Noah laughed, too. "Trust me, if I had graced the door of this place with any of those women, this place would've crumbled like Jericho."

"Noah Litchfield!" a voice from behind them called out. Maddie looked up to see a small, black man, dressed in a white and blue seersucker suit, and blue bow tie, approaching their table. Noah stood up and reached to shake the man's hand.

"Simon, my friend, it's good to see you!" Noah *was* happy to see him. "Thank you for the last minute accommodations. I owe you a huge return favor."

"Nonsense. I'm always glad to make exceptions for you and your family. Always good to have you, Noah. How have you been? Your parents?"

"Good, Simon, real good. We're all doing great."

"That's great to here. Now, my, my, you good man, who is this beautiful belle gracing your side this evening and why haven't you introduced us?" Simon reached for Maddie's hand.

"Simon, this is our new town physician, Dr. Madison Blaylock. Maddie, this is Simon Salley, proprietor of The Veranda." Noah introduced the two.

"Dr. Blaylock," Simon took Maddie's hand and kissed the top of it. "Welcome to Canton Cope and welcome to The Veranda. It is truly an honor to meet you."

"Thank you, Simon. Likewise and I must tell you, your restaurant is breathtaking. It compares to nothing I've seen before." Maddie said.

Simon bowed his head in a grateful gesture and replied, "Ah, even more breathtaking tonight for it has been host to the most lovely care-giver the Cope has ever had."

"Well now, I know why Noah and you are such good friends." Maddie laughed.

"Doctor, I am a true Southern gentleman and I can assure you the truth is the only thing to pass from these lips," Simon attested, smiling. "And Noah Litchfield is as honest a man as I am, even if we both share a common flaw in that we enjoy gazing upon such a beautiful lady."

"Thank you, Simon. You're very kind," Maddie smiled.

"Well now, " Simon glanced at his watch, "I

need to check on my chefs and make sure they're not trying to outdo my skills. You two enjoy your dinner and if I may, let me recommend the swordfish tonight. It's stuffed with a wonderful cream broccoli sauce and it is divine, if I must say so myself." He excused himself and headed toward the kitchen, which was located in the former basement of the house.

Sweet Dreams, Doc

CHAPTER EIGHT

Noah and Maddie enjoyed the stuffed swordfish with petal pastries of Crabmeat Newburg and fresh stalks of cauliflower in a shrimp and deviled almonds sauce. They forgo dessert and opted for one more glass of red wine.

After sitting for almost two hours at their table, Noah took Maddie for a stroll around the grounds of the restaurant. He showed her the old slave quarters, now tiny museums of history, the stables, now used as storage, and what was left of the centuries-old rice flats. They found a swing, lazily swaying in the breeze, hanging from a large limb of one of the live oaks and sat down.

Maddie sighed as they relaxed back in the swing. "Noah, this place is so wonderful. I'd never want to leave if it was mine."

"I'm really glad you like it so much,

Maddie."

"I have to be honest with you, Noah. I really didn't expect to enjoy myself so much today...or tonight, for that matter."

"I'm glad you were wrong, Doc."

"Me, too."

"I really am a good person, you know. Maybe a little high strung once in a while, but basically good," Noah grinned.

"I never doubted that you were a good person, just..."

"A little wild?"

"A little."

"Maddie, I've always wanted to be a family man. To be a husband and a father, there just hasn't been much of a variety to choose from here. And honestly, I wouldn't know if there had been many choices. I guess I wasn't looking for anything meaningful because I wasn't ready. Wasn't ready to grow up, have any responsibility other than myself and sometimes even that's been questionable."

"Sometimes things change, Noah."

"Sometimes they do."

They swayed in the night air for a little longer, in silence. Eventually, reluctantly, Noah took her hand and said, "Let's get outa here." Maddie demanded to pick up the tab for dinner and won the battle after giving Noah a look that told him she meant business. "I told you I wanted to do this to thank you for today. Now let me..." As they floated on the ferry back to the Cope, the stars shone brightly above them and the moon lit up the ocean in a spectacular display.

"It's a beautiful night," Maddie commented,

looking up at the heavens.

"Yes, it is...for a lot of reasons." Maddie looked at Noah and his eyes caught hers with a melting glance. "Maddie," he continued, "I need to apologize to you for being so annoying these past few months."

"You haven't been annoying. Maybe a little persistent, but not annoying." He took her hand in his and lightly stroked it with his thumb.

"I've never been persistent before, you've just awestruck me. At first, and I'm being honest now, as bad as it's going to sound, at first, it was just a matter of seek and find, divide and conquer. Dating the gorgeous new doctor. I couldn't see beyond those green eyes and those Olympic legs. But I don't know, as time went by, I started to feel differently. I started seeing you as Maddie, the person. Your compassion, your intelligence, your humor, all of it and I'd never even looked for that before."

"Noah, I don't know how to respond to that...I, I haven't...", Maddie tried to find the words, but Noah stopped her.

"Let me get this out, Doc. By the time I realized what a fabulous person you were, that I wanted to get to know you for reasons other than your beauty, that maybe, just maybe I could have a real relationship with someone for the first time in my life, I had already made such an ass of myself, I was afraid I'd never get the chance."

Maddie leaned over and kissed Noah on the cheek. "I'm sorry, too, Noah."

"What on earth for?"

"Because. For a long time, I only saw you from the outside, too. This beautiful, wealthy man with an ego the size of the Atlantic. Women parading around him all the time and a big reputation for being a ladies' man. I never took the time to think you were someone that may be really worth getting to know."

"Maddie, I didn't give you any reason to think I was worth knowing. That's my fault."

"No, no it isn't. I was judging a book by its cover and you know what they say about that."

"So I suppose we both need to open these books, don't we?" Noah smiled.

"I think we already have..."

Noah walked Maddie to her door to say good-night. It was only a little after eleven so she asked him if he wanted to come in for a cup of coffee.

"I think I'll pass tonight, Doc. Not that I wouldn't love to, but I want to do this the right way. The proper way. *The way my Daddy taught me*," Noah chuckled, imitating his father. "I don't want either of us put in a situation to do something before we're ready to."

Maddie smiled up at Noah. "I am surprised at you, Litchfield. Pleasantly surprised. There really is a side of you I didn't know existed."

"You bring out the best in me, Doc." He took her face in his hands, leaned down and kissed her softly. When she reached up and ran her hand through his hair, he pulled her tighter to him, kissing her ever so slightly harder. After a few tender seconds, he pulled back, kissing her cheek.

"Whew. That was beyond nice," Noah sighed. "Thank you for today, tonight, this very second. It was a special night for me and I owe it all to you."

"Thank you. I had a wonderful time. I wish we had done this sooner now, but that's my fault."

"We've got a lot of time to catch up, okay?" Noah assured her, brushing his hand along her neck and down her back.

"I know."

He kissed her quickly, one last time, and turned to go. "Goodnight, gorgeous. I'll call you tomorrow. Sweet dreams, Doc."

After running a hot bath, Maddie settled in the tub to relax and unwind. Her night with Noah had left her hyped up, to say the least. God, he was such a gentleman and nothing like she thought he'd be. On the other hand, when he had kissed her, a big part of her wanted him to take her right then and there and have his way with her. She couldn't remember when she'd been so aroused by one kiss, from any other man in her life.

CHAPTER NINE

Maddie headed to the square Sunday morning for church services. As she walked along the cobbled sidewalk, she could hear the church bells tolling in the distance. It was sunny and warm and the birds were singing...'*gosh, I'm starting to sound like a love song...what is wrong with me?'* But she knew. She was still floating from her date with Noah last night. Maddie couldn't stop smiling, although the little voice in her head kept telling her not to listen to her heart *'and quit smiling, for Pete's sake, you look like an idiot.'*

She spoke with several of the townspeople in the vestibule before making her way to a pew in the middle of the church. As she browsed through the morning's program, she heard someone ask her, "Is this seat taken?" She looked up to see Noah smiling down at her.

"Of course not, Noah." Her heart gave a little flutter. "Please, sit down." She slid over to make room for him.

"Good morning, my lady," Noah leaned over and kissed her cheek.

"Good morning, you," Maddie smiled back.

"Are you surprised?"

"Surprised that Jericho isn't crumbling at this very moment?" she giggled. "Yes, I am. I've been coming here for months and this is the first time I've seen you here."

"This is my church. I've been a member since I was nine. I just haven't been in a while. I guess I kind of let other things come first."

"Well, I'm glad you're here now."

"Me, too."

It was obvious after church, that the good people of Canton Cope had noticed the coupling of Noah and Maddie. They were all abuzz trying to nonchalantly watch them; Maddie and Noah couldn't help but be amused at their curiosity.

"Maddie, I see my parents, " Noah said. "Let's go over and say hello."

"Sure, I'd love to meet them."

They walked over to where Noah's parents were standing under a pecan tree talking to another older couple. Kirkland Litchfield reminded Maddie of that older actor, something Sutherland, she couldn't remember his first name, but had seen him in all of those old war movies her father loved to watch. Jestine Litchfield was a dead ringer for the lady that starred in The Graduate, the one that had seduced that college boy, only Mrs. Litchfield was an older version of the seductress. They were a handsome couple, impeccably dressed.

"Noah, my darling!" his mother kissed his cheek. "We saw you come into the service, we're so glad you came this morning."

"Hello, Mother."

"My good boy, how are you?" his father shook Noah's hand and hugged him.

"Good, Dad." Noah turned to Maddie. "Mother, Dad, this is Dr. Madison Blaylock, the Cope's new doctor. Maddie, these are my parents, Kirkland and Jestine Litchfield." Maddie shook their hands.

"It's so nice to meet both of you."

"Doctor? My, my, how wonderful to have such a young, vibrant physician in the Cope. I'd heard you were here, but thank heavens, I haven't had any ailments that needed fixing. I should have stopped by anyway to welcome you, but at my age,

I forget what day of the week it is. Welcome, Dr. Blaylock, to our little paradise," Jestine smiled warmly.

"And even more wonderful to see my son at your side," Kirkland was pleased.

"Thank you both. You're very kind. And I am very happy to be here," Maddie said.

"I'm surprised that Noah's antics haven't frightened you away yet, Dr. Blaylock," Kirkland stated, bluntly.

"Thank you, Father, for those words of praise. Shall I let her see my horns now, or save that for later?" Noah was smiling.

"Mr. Litchfield, your son is quite a charming young man. But I think you'd be very surprised to know he's been a perfect southern gentleman since the day I've met him. You raised him well,"

Maddie defended Noah.

Kirkland and Jestine smiled as Noah put his arm around Maddie and gave his parents a smile and a wink. “See there, Dad. I can be exactly what you’ve always wanted me to be...proper and refined.”

“Why don’t you two join us for lunch? We’ve plenty?” Jestine asked.

“Yes, Noah. Do come along. You and I have some business to discuss as well and today looks like a good day to do just that. What do you say?” Kirkland extended his own invitation.

“Well, I don’t have any plans. Maddie?” Noah asked.

“No, I was just going to have a sandwich. No special plans. But I’d love to join you,” she smiled at the Litchfields.

“Then it’s settled,” Noah confirmed. “we’ll

be there shortly."

"Would you like to ride with me?" Noah offered after his parents had left.

"Actually, I'd like to walk with you. It's such a pretty day, let's walk!"

"Doc, I can't resist that smile. Whatever the lady desires," he took her hand and they started down the cobbled walk.

"Your parents are great," Maddie said after they had walked for a moment or two.

"Yeah, they are. I don't know how in the world they ended up with three misfits like the twins and me."

"Noah, stop talking like that. It's obvious your parents love you very much."

"They do. I know that. But I wasn't

married by twenty-five with two point five kids. They just can't seem to get past that. Look at my brother and sister, for example. Julian married a girl from up north, they both screw around on each other and don't think anything of it. As long as Celeste, that's Julian's wife by the way, has the Litchfield name, she doesn't care what Julian does. And as long as Julian has his beloved Mrs. Julian Kirkland Litchfield, III, by his side for all of his social functions, he doesn't give a shit what she does." Noah scratched his head and shrugged his shoulders. "I don't even know if they love each other."

"What a life, " Maddie sighed.

"Ah, then there's Julia, lord help that woman. She let that stupid idiot, Tucker Donovan, talk her into marrying him. That he loved her." Noah laughed sarcastically. "He loved her last name. She does nothing all day but watch soap operas and gossip; waiting for Tucker to come home. Meanwhile, he's usually down at the Cotton Club, drinking like a fish, and taking up with any sea witch that'll have him. Poor, dumb, Julia thinks he's out working like a dog." Noah paused, thinking of his brother and sister. "And you know the funny thing?" Maddie shook her head. "My parents think Julian and Julia have perfect lives. They wonder why I didn't get married by twenty-five. Damn, that's about as sorry a life as I can imagine."

"I had no idea about either of them." Maddie looked up at Noah, a little saddened by the thought of having such a life. "Now I know why you're worried about the business."

"Well, I've been thinking about that, too. About what you said and trusting my father to do the right thing. No matter who is left in charge, I'll still always own a third of Litchfield and the shares. The twins can't do anything without my knowledge or consent." Noah continued, " As long as Donovan doesn't do anything to cause the business to fold, I think Julian and I can pretty much keep things in tow. And if Julian is given presidential rights to oversee the daily operations, I know, without a doubt, he'll keep me in charge. He doesn't want the job, just the authority. Regardless, my relationship with Dad won't change, no matter what he chooses to do."

Maddie smiled at Noah. "I'm proud of you, Noah. That's a very mature attitude to have."

"Kinda scary, ain't it?" Noah laughed.

CHAPTER TEN

Some twenty minutes later, they arrived at the Litchfield home and as they rounded the corner into the back garden, Noah saw Julia's and Tucker's Cadillac parked in the drive. "Great. The freeloaders are here, " he turned to Maddie. "Please don't judge my parents, or me, by those two. I'm just preparing you. It isn't going to be pleasant." Noah smirked.

"Noah, please, quit being so cynical," Maddie told him.

They walked into the massive foyer and made their way into the living room. The house was as beautiful as Maddie imagined it would be. It would have placed a very close second in any competition with The Veranda. The only difference in the Litchfield house was that it was a home in every since of the word. Family photos were everywhere, as well as many of Jestine's collections of depression glass and antique sewing boxes. Maddie noticed Mr. Litchfield was a collector of smoking pipes and compasses. Kirkland and Jestine were seated with glasses of lemonade and Julia was standing at the fireplace babbling about something of no importance.

"Noah, Dr. Blaylock, come in!" Kirkland stood up with a show of southern respect.

"Would ya'll like a glass of lemonade, it's so humid out. I swear I can't breathe out there today," Jestine offered. She poured two glasses of ice and lemonade and offered them to Noah and Maddie as Noah introduced his sister to the doctor.

"Maddie, this is my sister, Julia Litchfield-Donovan. Julia, this is Dr. Blaylock."

"Doctor? Hmmmmm, you look awfully young to be a doctor. How long have you been practicing?" Julia quizzed. Before Maddie could defend herself, Noah stepped in.

"Julia, she's not too young to be a doctor. Maddie just happened to have had the desire to do something meaningful with her life instead of becoming a gossiping do-gooder. Her hands are skilled far beyond that of working a remote control. Which is what you do best!"

"Noah, " Maddie tried to interrupt him.

"Julia, Noah, now I won't stand for you two bickering today. We have a guest and I won't have it," Kirkland reprimanded his children.

"I'm sorry, Dad," Noah apologized.

"Of course she's *old* enough to be a doctor." Julia chimed in. "I've heard all the talk around town, though, and we just can't believe someone so pretty, would have the *brains* to be a doctor." Then she giggled.

Noah bristled. “Julia, I swear you do *not* want to push me today!”

Kirkland intervened. “Julia, this is my home. If you don’t respect my wishes, and mind your manners, show Dr. Blaylock the hospitality she deserves, you’ll have to leave. Now I’ve spoken and you will apologize.”

“I apologize,” Julia said flatly, rolling her eyes at her father.

“Julia, come with me,” Jestine suggested. “Let’s check on Mamie and see if we can help her with lunch.”

Kirkland sat back in his chair after his wife and daughter left the room and offered his apologies to Maddie. “Dr. Blaylock, please forgive Julia. She’s a little spoiled and naive to the ways of the world, so to speak. I imagine she’s probably a little envious of your success.”

"Naive, hell. She's lived with Donovan too damn long," Noah grumbled. "Where is my imbecile of a brother-in-law anyway?"

Kirkland shook his head in dismay, "He's in the den watching the game."

"Come on Maddie, let me introduce you to the jellybean," Noah said flatly.

Tucker was stretched out on the leather sofa with the remote control in one hand, and a bag of potato chips in the other, crumbs covering his enormous belly and chest.

"You never pass up a free meal, do you, Donovan?" Noah implied.

Tucker smiled a sarcastic, partially toothless grin. "Tata chip, Litch?"

"Wouldn't want to ruin my appetite, though you're doing a pretty good job of ruining it for me,"

Noah said.

"Who's the babe?" Tucker drooled, not bothering to stand.

"Dr. Madison Blaylock, the new doctor. Maddie, this is Tucker Donovan, my brother-in-law."

Tucker laughed. "Doctor of *what*?"

Noah glared at Tucker. "God, where are your manners, Tuck?"

"Sorry there, Mizzz Blaylock," Tucker sneered. "But let me tell ya something, okay? Noah here, ain't after ya for ya brains, you do know that, don't ya?"

"Tucker, actually," Maddie spoke up before Noah blew a fuse, "I'm not after him for his brains either." She leaned over Tucker ever so seductively and whispered in his ear. "He can make love for hours on end and I just can't get enough of him.

Who cares if he's as dumb as a box of rocks? Look at him. I'm in it for the sex, but let's keep that our little secret, okay?" Tucker's face was on fire, as he hung on every word she said and Noah thought his sides would split from not laughing out loud.

"Well, now," Noah cleared his throat, "I'm glad you cleared that up, Maddie. Any more questions, Donovan?"

Tucker swallowed hard and barely mumbled, "Uh, no...Noah, no."

They managed to get through lunch peacefully. After dessert, Noah and Maddie snuck away to the third floor porch overlooking the ocean.

"You grew up in a beautiful home, Noah, " Maddie complimented.

"I'm proud of it. I'm quite proud of my parents, too. Julia...well, that's another story. I'm so embarrassed at the way she and Donovan behaved today. I really, truly am sorry you had to deal with them."

"Please don't apologize," she brushed her hand down Noah's back. "Julia acts that way because of Tucker. I know she wasn't raised that way. When you live with someone for so long, and put all of your love and trust into that one person, regardless of how unhealthy that relationship may be, a person can literally become an extension of that. She's simply become an extension of Tucker."

"I just wanted today to be so nice for you..."

"I've been with you and your parents all afternoon, how could it not have been nice?"

"You flatter me...."

Kirkland emerged through the French doors, excusing himself for interrupting them.

"Noah, son, might I steal a moment from you, if your Bella grants me permission? We've some business to discuss."

"Of course, Dad. Maddie, if you'll excuse me..."

"Certainly. I'll just enjoy the view, take your time, I'll be fine," Maddie said.

"I won't be too long," Noah whispered as he kissed her cheek.

Shortly after Noah went inside with his father, Jestine joined Maddie on the porch .

"May I join you, honey?" she asked.

"Absolutely, Mrs. Litchfield. Please do..."

"It's such a lovely view, isn't it?" Jestine asked, rocking gently in a large, white rocking chair.

Sweet Dreams, Doc

"It's breathtaking. How wonderful it must be to wake up each morning to this horizon," Maddie stated.

"Unfortunately, after forty years here, we've started taking this view for granted. We've hardly slowed down to just sit and enjoy it.

"You've been greatly rewarded, though, for that hard work. Litchfield Shrimp is the main supplier for most of the southeastern coast; that kind of growth doesn't come easily."

"No it hasn't, and that's why I'm so pleased Kirkland is ready to pass it down. I'm so ready to retire and see some of this fine world."

CHAPTER ELEVEN

Noah sat with his father in the library, knowing what was to come; the moment of truth. His father was just before telling him which of the three Litchfield children would take over the business. Noah couldn't help but wonder what he would do if it wasn't him. *'No matter what,'* Maddie's words echoed in his mind, *'don't ruin your relationship with your father.'*

"Son, I must say to begin with, your Dr. Blaylock is most lovely. You seem quite smitten with her."

"Dad, I am taken with her. She's so unlike any other woman I've ever been with. I am completely fascinated with her."

"She is certainly different from the others in the fact that *she*, my dear boy, is a *lady*!"

Noah laughed. "Yes, Father. She is a lady in

every aspect of the word."

"Ahh, Noah, I am very pleased with your desire to surround yourself with such a refined woman. Your mother and I have spent countless hours distressed over your past *affairs*." Kirkland walked over to the wet bar. "Brandy?"

"Yes, sir. Thank you."

Kirkland poured two snifters and returned to his leather wing-back chair.

"I have many regrets, Dad, in my life. The main one being I have disappointed you and Mother with my careless lifestyle. I am sorry for any embarrassment I have caused you."

"Nonsense, boy! Your lifestyle has never done more than concern me. You're a fine man, Noah, and we are very proud of you. We're proud of the way you represent Litchfield, the way you have developed outstanding business relationships with our markets and especially the way you have respected and looked out for our employees." Kirkland's face suddenly grew sullen. "My shame lies in your brother and sister."

"I don't understand..." Noah was baffled.

"It is no secret, Noah, that your mother thinks the twins are perfect. Blind love, blind as hell if you ask me." Kirkland shook his head. "I do *not* share her opinion."

"You don't?" Noah was noticeably shocked.

"Good god, boy, I'm not an idiot! I simply keep my mouth shut to make your mother happy. It's as if Julian doesn't exist and sometimes I wish Julia lived up north with him, too. That damned moron, Donovan, makes my blood boil. I don't know why in the hell I ever consented to that marriage. All three of them have used the

Litchfield name to better themselves in ways you and I have done simply with hard work. Julian used it to become a socialite and your sister and Tucker have used to parade around this town like royalty."

Noah made no comment, either to agree or disagree. His father obviously needed to vent, and from the sounds of it, had needed to do so for a very long time. He gave his father the respect to do just that.

"Enough of this foolishness. Noah, you know I'm an old man. I'm tired, I've exhausted myself with this business of ours and I'm past ready to hand this responsibility over to someone else." He slowly raised himself from his chair and walked over to the mammoth cherry desk and unlocked a drawer, removing a leather portfolio.

"Son, your mother and I have done some serious contemplating over this matter these past months. I've made my decision and your mother stands by that decision, and by me. Your brother has been made aware of my decision and I have his appropriate signatures on these documents. I have not, as of yet, enlightened Julia." Noah held his breath as his father continued. "In my hands, within these documents, you will find everything has been filed with my attorneys and there will be no changes. Do you understand, son?"

"Yes sir." Noah nodded.

"Very well then. As of today, with your signature, Noah, this establishment will be in your full command."

Noah stood from his chair and approached the desk. "Father, I don't know what to say. Are you certain I am the one to do this?" His heart was racing. Kirkland lifted his hand in protest.

"Listen to me carefully, Noah. There will be no questions asked, no further discussions. I have made my decision. You have stood by me for thirty-five years, from the time you could walk you've been by my side on a trawler. You've worked hard and you never doubted me, my business decisions or my methods of production. There was never a time I doubted you or questioned your ability to take my place. Understood?"

"Yes, Dad. Thank you for trusting me to do this." Kirkland handed Noah his ink pen and slid the documents across the desk within Noah's reach. Noah signed his name eleven times, his mind spinning with each signature. When he finished, he shook hands with and embraced his father.

"I'll make you proud of me, Dad. I'll be honest and fair and Litchfield Shrimp will continue to run exactly the way it has for almost a century, the way Grandfather started it. I give you my word."

"Son, I'm already proud of you and I've no

doubts that you'll keep your word." Kirkland patted his son on the back. "Well now, the time's come to inform your sister and brother-in-law of this matter."

"Dad, how on earth did Julian agree to this?"

"Noah, your brother has no interest in running this company. As long as he makes a profit from his shares, he could care less who runs it. There was never a question, when I proposed this to him. He never raised an eyebrow. Donovan, on the other hand, will have something to say about it. However, I don't give a rat's ass what he has to say. He married into this family, and into this business, much to my regret, but he will have no authority over its operations."

****

Kirkland had Mamie call the others into the

living room while he fetched a bottle of champagne from the cellar. When he returned, all were waiting on him. Noah, with Maddie at his side, Jestine seated proudly before him and Julia and Tucker, each with a slice of cake in their hands.

"Ooooo, Daddy! Champagne! I smell excitement in the air. Is it good news?" Julia squealed.

"Yes, my dear, very good news."

Maddie looked at Noah, who only winked at her in reply. Kirkland popped open the bottle and filled everyone's glasses.

"My dear family, our special guest Dr. Blaylock, I would like to make a toast. In my hand I have the Articles of Incorporation for Litchfield Shrimp. They have been endorsed by Jestine, Julian, Noah and myself. As of today, Litchfield Shrimp comes under the command of Noah Reed Litchfield. Here, here!" He raised his glass in a toast.

"What?!" Tucker choked on his cake.

"Daddy?!" Julia wailed.

Maddie threw her arms around Noah's neck and kissed him.

"Julia, you know very well," Kirkland stated, "Noah is the only one of the three of you capable of keeping Litchfield in the manner in which it has been run for nearly a century. Tucker will continue to captain the first fleet, but his authority ends there. Your signature on these documents will insure he keeps that job so long as you are married to him. If there is any disagreement on your or his part, he can find a job elsewhere. Understood?"

"Yes, Daddy," Julia sobbed.

"Donovan?" Kirkland looked at Tucker.

"Whatever. Ain't gotta like it though," Tucker grumbled and walked out of the house.

Julia reluctantly signed the papers and went after Tucker, sniffling. Jestine rose from her seat to embrace her son. "I'm very proud of you, Noah. I'm confident your father has made the right decision."

"Thank you, Mother."

"Son," Kirkland warned, "I think it's safe to say that we haven't heard the last of Tucker's disappointment."

"I agree, Dad. He's going to be more of a trouble maker now than ever before."

Kirkland advised, "Just be on your guard and watch your back. I'm not concerned with the crew; they all admire and respect you and I don't feel there will be any problems from them. Donovan, on the other hand, will take every opportunity to start trouble. It'll take a few weeks, but I feel sure he'll adjust. Until then, just keep your eyes and your ears open."

"If there's any repercussions on his part, I'll handle it," Noah said.

Jestine added, "Just try and remember he is your sister's husband."

****

As they walked back to the church to get Noah's car, he was floating on a cloud.

"Are you okay?" Maddie asked, smiling.

"I'm great! Today has been such a relief for me. I've been so consumed with this for weeks, I've lost sleep over it, and I've thought of little else...it's just a huge weight off my shoulders."

"I think it's wonderful. Now you can relax a

little and be happy that your parents are going to be able to slow down and enjoy the rest of their lives," Maddie said.

"And what about that with you and Tucker?!" Noah laughed. "My god, I thought I would burst a seam I was trying so hard not to laugh! He was all but melting on that sofa...I think you probably shut him up for good."

"I just gave him what he wanted, told him what he wanted to hear..."

"Oh yeah, and then some!"

After retrieving Noah's car, the two of them sat down on the hill below Maddie's house to watch the sun go down. "I'm proud of you, you know," Maddie softly said. "You've shown me the real Noah Litchfield and I'm very glad I've met him."

"I don't know whether I've done a lot of growing up in the past few months, or whether I've just chosen to finally prove that I'm better than that. I know I've come to realize that my life was more of racing wide open, never looking back and not caring what the next day held. In that I've also come to realize that's no way to live. Life is too short to spend it chasing each day."

"No, I prefer relishing in each day. Don't get me wrong, Noah. I race through my days sometimes, too, but I also enjoy the days where I can just sit back and wonder about the future and what my goals are. Losing my parents helped me learn to live each and every day as if it were my last on earth."

"Yes, m'am, I'm looking forward to spending some days living like there was no tomorrow and doing it all with you." Noah smiled. "You know if you'd said yes the first time I asked you out, what almost a year ago now, we might even be married by now? We sure have a hell of a lot of catching up to do."

"If I had said yes back then, I'd probably have never gone out with you again. I didn't *know* you back then like I do now. You'd have had to hog tie me to get me to go out with you!" Maddie laughed.

"That could've been arranged," Noah laughed back, leaning onto Maddie and giving her a little nudge.

"So what do you think about Tucker? Do you think he's going to be a problem?" Maddie asked.

"There's no telling what kind of crap he'll try to pull."

"Just be careful with him, Noah. He looks like he can get pretty angry when he wants to and I don't want you crossing paths with him."

"Well, Doc, we're going to cross paths, I

mean we work together. And he can get extremely violent when he wants to, but I've got a crew of nearly fifty men that regard him as an asshole. He won't push too far, before they start pushing back."

"Promise me you won't provoke him?"

"Maddie," Noah smiled, "are you worried about me?"

"Kind of," she smiled back, "yes, I'm a little worried."

Noah kissed her softly and hugged her. "Little lady, now more than ever, I have every reason to keep my head on straight. I've been given the command of Litchfield and I've met the woman I've been looking for all my life. I'm not about to do anything to end either of those, okay?"

"Good answer." They kissed again and Noah said goodnight.

Sweet Dreams, Doc

CHAPTER TWELVE

The next few weeks went by quietly. Maddie quickly became close friends with Noah's parents and had enjoyed several evenings at their home. She'd even had them to her home for supper on a few occasions. Periodically, she'd see Julia and Tucker, and so far, each visit had been peaceful. Awkward, but peaceful.

Moby was like a kid at Christmas when she learned Maddie had finally gone out with Noah; totally excited and relieved that her best friend really hadn't been dropped on her head as a baby. She had visited the Cope on many weekends and had become fast friends with Noah.

Moby's only regret was that he hadn't asked her out first. "You know you owe me one, Noah. You let me down, put me out in left field with no glove. You've got to redeem yourself...find me a man!" she joked. Noah assured Moby he'd do his best, but she needed to be patient. "There aren't many out there like me, Moby. This may take some time." He winked at her.

****

Noah left the docks close to eight o'clock. The shrimping season was winding down and he was working later every day trying to get in as much shrimp as he could. He always liked to push the envelope towards the end of the season, it made for a nice bonus for the guys. A little extra to tide them over until next year. Maddie wasn't home yet and he wondered where she would be at that hour. As he drove down the drive way to his cottage, Noah smiled when he saw Maddie's Civic parked under the house.

His home was a typical beach home. Cedar siding clapboard, screened in front porch, and a dock walk from the house straight down to the water. It was definitely a bachelor's haven with rustic furniture, heart of pine paneled walls, all decorated in masculine earth tones. Fishing, crabbing and shrimping paraphernalia strewn everywhere, it was a man's home to say the least, but spotless. Noah was quite the neat freak.

When he opened the jeep door, the aroma of charcoal tempted his nostrils. He walked into the backyard and saw Maddie standing over the grill up on the deck. "What's all this?" Noah smiled up at her.

"Hey sweetie. Rare, right?"

Noah laughed, "Rare," nodding his head. He walked up the stairs to the deck and drew her to him. After a quick kiss and some playful butt-grabbing, Noah finally said simply, "Hi."

"Hi, yourself."

“This is a nice surprise.”

“I thought you’d like to come home and find supper waiting on you.”

“ I kind of like coming home and finding you waiting for me.”

“I kind of like that, too.” Maddie grinned.

“Have I got time for a shower?”

“Yep, the salad and potatoes are done, but the steaks need a few more minutes. Go ahead and get cleaned up.”

An hour later, with full bellies and a cleaned kitchen, they settled on the sofa. Noah had started a fire in the fireplace and they were cuddled in front of it.

“So how are things going with Tucker?” Maddie asked.

“Tense, still. He bristles at the sight of

me."

"Your mom called me at the office today. Seems Julia and he had another fight. She wanted me to talk with Julia."

"Doc, please don't get involved in their problems. I don't want Tucker to have any reason to harass you."

"I just thought I'd take her to lunch, see how she's doing. Maybe get her to open up to me, tell me what's going on."

"You know, Maddie, she wasn't always this way." Noah remembered. "I mean, she was well-raised, proper, and lady-like. She could have had any man in this town, beautiful...just beautiful. She was homecoming queen, prom queen, extremely popular. Everything. But she got her heart broke by some guy while she was still in college and never really got over that. Julia came home after graduating, didn't have a clue what she wanted to do with her life. She didn't want a regular job, she didn't want a spectacular job; she didn't want much of anything." Maddie just nodded. She knew what it was like to have your heart broken, she'd had hers torn apart a couple of times herself.

Noah continued, "Then she met Tucker and she went even further downhill from there. She thinks everyone in this town is jealous of her, when the truth is, they're all making fun of her. It just kills me. She's not the sister I grew up with."

"I feel so sorry for her, Noah," Maddie declared. "She's not had a chance to really be herself being married to Tucker. I know heartbreak and I can see her falling hard for the first man to show her any attention after being heartbroken. Unfortunately, that person was Tucker."

"I used to feel sorry for her, I felt like she was caught up in a situation she had no control over. But all she had to do was leave the bastard. She has nothing to lose and everything to gain. But..." Noah's words hung in the air, "Julia thinks the sun rises and sets on Tucker and I don't have a clue how to make her see him for what he is."

At that exact moment, a loud pounding on the front door, startled them. "Open the damn door, Litchfield, you son-of-a-bitch!" Noah sprung to his feet, threw open the door and found Tucker on the other side, in a fit of rage.

"Donovan, what in the hell is wrong with you?!"

"You sorry bastard!" Tucker swung his fist to hit Noah. Noah, moving quickly, ducked to avoid the punch and threw Tucker to the floor, knocking over a lamp in the process. Maddie jumped up and moved to the other side of the room, getting out of their way. Tucker struggled to his feet, obviously drunk, and wiped his frothing mouth.

"Who the *hell* do you think you are?!" Noah roared. Tucker raised his arm to attempt another blow at Noah, only to be met with a solid punch squarely on the jaw. The punch sent Tucker rolling over the sofa, but he wasn't done trying. He wiped blood from his lip and bent down, charging at Noah like a bull. Noah stepped aside and came up behind him, locking his arm around Tucker's neck.

"Tuck, I don't know what your *fucking* problem is, ughh," Noah groaned as he tightened his grip, "but, if you *ever* barge in *my* damn house again, *I'll fuckin' kill you*!" He pushed Tucker to the floor. "You smell like a goddamn brewery! Get up!" Noah kicked Tucker in the back side. *"GET UP!"*

"You think you so high and mighty," Tucker wiped more blood and spit from his swollen lip, "fucking the good doctor. I bet she tastes really good, too."

Noah grabbed Tucker by the neck and threw him against the wall, sending a rack of fishing rods to the floor and held him there. *"Damn you, you low-life, piece of shit!"* Noah roared again, through his clenched teeth. "Keep your filthy mouth shut. *Don't* you *ever* look at her again. If I ever so much as see you *glance* her way again, *I will fuckin' rip your eyeballs out with my bare hands and shove them so far up your ass, you'll be looking at your insides the rest of your damned life!"*

"I'll ruin you, Noah, " Tucker whispered. "I'll take everything you got. Don't turn your back for one second, cause you'll lose it all. *Everything...,*" Tucker said looking at Maddie once again. That was the final straw. Noah's rage blew full speed ahcad and he let loose a series of punches and blows that would have put Tucker in a coma had Maddie not stepped in.

"Noah! Noah! Stop it! You're going to kill him!" She pulled on Noah's arm, trying in vain to get him to stop.

"You stupid son-of-a-bitch! I will make your life a fucking hell!" Noah was screaming at Tucker while he continued to pummel him.

"*NOAH!"* Maddie screamed. "You're going to kill him!" Noah turned then, and looked at Maddie with eyes full of hate and pure unabashed rage. "Then let me kill the motherfucker!," he bellowed at her, scaring her.

"Noah..." Maddie said softly, and took a couple of steps back.

Noah's eyes immediately cleared and Maddie came into focus. "Maddie, honey, god, I'm sorry. I'm so sorry. I didn't mean to yell at you..." He put his arms around her tightly.

Noah then picked Tucker up and threw him down the front steps. Tucker landed in a heap near his pick-up truck. “Follow me to Julia’s, Doc. I’m going to drive this fucker home.” He picked Tucker up again and threw him in the back of Tucker’s truck and headed to his sister’s house with Maddie behind him in the jeep. Noah laid on the horn when he pulled in Julia’s drive. He was dragging Tucker from the back of the truck when Julia came running down the porch. “Get your damn hands off me,” Tucker grumbled to Noah.

“Noah?” Julia cried. “What’s wrong with Tuck?”

“He’s drunk, Julia. What does it look like?”

“Oh, Tuck, baby. Come on in the house and let me clean you up, sweetie,” she crooned, helping Tucker up the steps.

“Damn, Julia! How can you put up with this

shit? How can you live with this no good bastard? Look at him!" Noah was as angry with Julia as he was with Tucker.

"Because he's my husband and I love him. Don't you dare talk about him that way!"

"Your *husband* just barged into my house and proceeded to attack me. Only I beat the shit out of him first. You keep him away from me, Julia, or you're going to find yourself a widow. You got that, Julia? Keep him the *fuck* away from me!"

"Noah, he just got carried away, that's all. He's been upset about Litchfield and all, you know. He was really disappointed."

"Don't make excuses for him. There is no excuse for the bastard. Why don't you just kick the SOB out? Why, *goddammit*, do you put up with his *shit?"*

Julia was crying, "Noah, please. He's my

husband."

Noah was shaking his head back and forth. "You don't have a clue, do you, Julia?" He turned and left his sister standing there crying.

Maddie sat in the car while Noah confronted Julia. The whole thing had shaken her badly. Tucker was completely out of control, vile, evil even and she had seen pure hatred in Noah's eyes. By the time Noah got in the car, she was visibly trembling. Noah let out a heavy sigh as he started the car. "I'm sorry you had to see that, Maddie."

"It's okay. I just hate it happened."

Noah looked over at Maddie and saw she was trembling and had tears running down her face. "God, baby...you're shaking," he said as he pulled her into his arms. She fell into his chest like a small, frightened child. "That bastard pushed me too far, tonight, Maddie... when he looked at you the way he did, I wanted to kill him with my bare hands."

"He scared me so badly..." Maddie sniffed. "I was so afraid of what was going to happen, of what *did* happen."

Noah held her tightly and wiped a tear from her cheek. "He's never going to bother you again. I will spend the rest of my life keeping him away from you. If it means killing him, he will stay the hell away from you."

"Noah, please, just stay away from him, too. I don't know what I'd do if something happened to you."

"Doc, he might be a big man, but when he's drinking, he's a total pussy. And he doesn't have the balls to come after me when he's sober." Noah started the jeep and grimaced as he shifted the gear in reverse. "Damn."

"Your hand?"

"Yeah, I think I cut my knuckle."

"I'll look at it when we get to the house." She picked up his hand and kissed it gently.

Noah leaned over and kissed her, "let's go home," he whispered.

Sweet Dreams, Doc

CHAPTER THIRTEEN

Maddie washed Noah's hand with peroxide after getting home. It was only bruised and had a tiny cut on it.

"Your boo-boo doesn't even need a band-aid. Just a little TLC. It'll probably be sore for a day or two....," she kissed each finger of Noah's hand, "but I think you'll still be able to use it."

She took one of his fingers, slid it in her mouth and rolled her tongue around it and then slowly slipped it from her lips. "You might want to exercise it frequently, though..." she said softly in his ear.

Noah pulled Maddie onto his lap and ran his free hand up her back. "What kind of exercise does the doctor prescribe?"

"Multiple flexing....," she whispered.

"Yeah?"

"Some full hand stroking might help..."

"Sounds like a work-out."

"Guaranteed results, though."

Noah leaned down and caught Maddie in an open mouth, heated kiss. She welcomed it with parted lips and passionately sucked his tongue. Noah's hands cradled her breasts and found her hard nipples. He groaned with pleasure as her hand slid between his legs and massaged his hard cock. Noah lifted his hands and took Maddie's in his own, looking into her eyes. "Maddie, I know you wanted to take things slow, but I want to *make love* to you. More than I've *ever* wanted to before." His voice was hoarse with desire.

"*Then don't stop*," she whispered back They moved to the rug in front of the fire, removing each other's clothes on the way. They wasted no time.

Noah caressed Maddie's body with his hands, while his tongue delved into places unknown. She did her own caressing, consuming every inch of him with her warm mouth and playfully whispering in his ear what she wanted him to do to her. It drove him crazy with desire. He entered her slowly, wanted to feel every single move and rode her in perfect rhythm as she wrapped her legs around him. As their passion grew, she climbed on top of him and just as she felt herself climaxing, Noah sat up and pulled her to him. As she trembled in his arms, he let go of himself and as he released his longing into her body, she climaxed again.

They collapsed in a bundle of arms and legs, both shaking and breathing hard. "Oh god, Maddie, I love you," Noah whispered, looking into her eyes. Maddie wrapped her arms around his neck and kissed him. "I love you," she whispered back. He held her for a long time, stroking her breasts with one hand and holding her hand with the other. She ran her fingers through the hair on his chest and fell asleep listening to his heart beat beneath her.

When she opened her eyes, it was near daybreak and she was alone. Maddie smelled coffee and smiled as she remembered the night before. As she pulled the blanket around her shoulders, Noah walked into the den.

“Good morning, handsome.”

“Good morning, Doc,” he said, as he knelt down to kiss her. “Come here.” He lifted her from the floor and put her in his lap. “About last night...” Noah started to say.

“Noah, it was wonderful...you were wonderful.”

“Maddie, I just want you to know, I’m sorry if I got a little carried away last night. I know you wanted to wait. But I swear to God and all that’s good, *I love you.* And I've never been in love before. I don't want you to get the wrong idea that now that we've made love, my conquest is over..." Maddie tried to stop him, but Noah placed a finger on her lips. "No, let me finish. It started out as a game for me, you know that. Before that night at The Veranda, I only wanted to sleep with you. You know that, too. But over these past months, I have fallen hopelessly in love with you. I don't even know when I realized it, but last night seemed like the right time to tell you."

"Noah, baby," she took his face in her hands and brushed his hair back from his face. "I stopped worrying about this being a game a long time ago. Once I came to know you and trust you the way I have, all of my fears went away. I realized a while back that I loved you, too, but I didn't know how you felt. And I didn't want to look like a fool by telling you that I loved you, if you didn't feel the same way."

He took her into his arms and they made love again as the sun continued to rise and the world woke up. Later they showered together and had coffee. Noah called down to the docks around seven o'clock to see if Tucker was at work yet.

"Yessa," Jasper answered. "He been hare 'round six. Look lak shit, too."

"Good, he ought to. I want you to tell him to go home. He isn't working today."

"Say what dere, boss?" Jasper was confused.

"*Tell him to go home*. He can lose a day's pay today."

"Galdamity, Noah, dat man gonna be shittin' wid you."

"Well, Jasper, let's just say he owes me a day's pay. That work for you?"

"Works fa me, dat shithead be in a mood already and I's ain't up fa none of hissin' shit today, no way. Ya's done me a favah, das for sho!"

"Thank you, Jasp. I'll see ya'll in a little while. If he gives you any shit, you call me."

"I's take great plesha in tellin' hissin' ass da go home. He don't be wantin' da start no shit wid me. Don' start no shit, won' be no shit, ain't dat right, boss?" Jasper laughed.

"That's right, Jasp. Hold down the fort. See you shortly." Noah laughed as he hung up the phone. *'God, I hope Donovan starts some shit with Jasper today. It'd be mighty funny to see him get his ass kicked twice in less than twelve hours,'* Noah thought as he found Maddie in the kitchen.

"So, good-looking...what time can I expect you tonight?" Maddie asked Noah.

"Oh, I don't know. How about I get some clothes together and let you take them with you when you leave. That way I can just come straight to you after work....like a B line. How's that sound?" Noah smiled.

"You read my mind....just remember your toothbrush," she grinned slyly.

"Oooo, lady, I like the way you think. Come here, " Noah moved toward her. "I love you."

"I love you," Maddie kissed him.

****

Noah pulled up at the harbor and was met at the door to the office by Jasper. The man was pissed.

"Noah, dat Tucker be in a mood dis mornin', all right all ready. He done tole me he ain't goin' no damn where. I's 'bout ready to kick hissin' ass back da whereba da hell he done come from! He cussin' up a storm and tellin' everbody da git da hell outa hissin' way."

"He's got a nasty hangover, Jasper, and I beat the hell out of him last night after he tried to tear down my house. I'll take care of him." Tucker was standing on the 'Miss Charlotte Jean', clipboard in hand, assigning navigation routes to his crew when Noah hopped aboard.

"How you feeling this morning, Donovan?" Noah said as loudly as he could. Tucker had a large bruise on his jaw and a cut on his lip.

"You gotta yell, asshole?" Tucker growled.

"You got a problem? You're supposed to be home." The crew all looked at each other and some shrugged their shoulders. They knew the two men hated each other and wasn't surprised to see them exchanging words.

"Yeah, what the hell is this shit? Since when do you tell me what to do?"

"Since you barged into my house and *tried* to beat the shit out of me. Which as all of you can see," Noah turned to the crew, "obviously didn't happen."

Tucker laughed. "Man, you gotta problem. So I got a little shit-faced last night, so what?"

"I'll tell you what...you've got a wife, thank god you've got no children, but you do have a wife, who for reasons I'll never know, loves you. Everything that you have is because of her. Instead of getting drunk and screwing around with some whore down at the Cotton Club, take your sorry ass home and spend some time with her. Be a goddamn man!" Noah turned to walk away and looked back. "And another thing, if you so much as raise your voice to me ever again, if you ever even *glance* at Maddie again, say one vile word to her, *I will kill you.* No jokes, no threats, that's a promise. You got that? Now go your ass home." Noah jumped down from the trawler and Tucker was right behind him.

"Like you gonna be able to keep her? Litchfield, that woman ain't enough for you and you know it. You'll be chasing that Wells bitch again in no time. And Maddie ain't gonna put up with that shit, she'll be gone, she ain't that kinda woman. I know the only reason you're with her in the first place. Impress the old man, 'get a decent woman and ole' daddy will give me the business'" Tucker told Noah.

In two strides, Noah was within an inch of Tucker's face. "You get this straight for the last time, Donovan. Maddie is everything I want and everything I'll ever want. It's called commitment, asshole, something you know nothing about. Now," Noah flipped the baseball cap from Tucker's head, "you keep your damn mouth shut and stay the hell away from me, my home and especially Maddie. And go home, goddammit!" Jasper stuck his head from the door of the office and called out, "Noah! Ya gots a phone call!" Noah waved his hand to let Jasper know he had heard him and looked back at Tucker, "*Get the hell out of here!*"

****

Just minutes before Noah's confrontation at the docks with Tucker, Caroline knocked on Maddie's office door. "Dr. Blaylock?", she said as she opened the door.

"Come on in, Caroline."

"Maddie, Julia's here to see you and she's pretty upset. Can you see her now?"

"How many patients are out front?"

"Only two."

"Okay, go ahead and take them to rooms two and four, have Alline check them out. I'll see them shortly. Where's Julia?"

"She's in the hall. She didn't want to stay in the waiting room." Maddie stepped into the hall and found Julia waiting near the back door. "Julia?"

"Maddie, I'm sorry to bother you. I didn't know else to go." She started to cry openly and was terribly shaken.

"Come on in. What's wrong?"

Julia followed Maddie into her office and sat down. "Maddie, I don't know what to do. He's going to kill me and I can't stop him."

"Julia, what are you talking about?"

Julia removed her sunglasses and Maddie gasped. Her left eye was black and swollen and her nose was bulging at the bridge.

"Julia, did *Tucker* do this to you?"

"I think my nose is broken!" Julia sobbed.

"Oh my god, Julia, *why*?"

"He was drunk last night."

"I'm well aware of that, but that doesn't justify *this! Nothing does!*"

"He was furious with Noah and took it out on me."

"*That bastard.*"

"Maddie, he hasn't always been this way. I don't know what's happened to him."

"Julia, you're going to press charges, aren't you?" Maddie asked, as she gingerly examined Julia's nose.

"*Charges*? God no! I'm his wife!" Julia

exclaimed.

"Exactly why he shouldn't be doing this. This isn't the first time, is it?"

Julia hesitated for a long time before she quietly replied ".....no."

"Alright, stay here. I'm going to get some bandages. *Don't* leave!" Maddie went straight to the front desk and called the harbor, praying Noah hadn't gone out yet.

"Hello?" Noah picked up the phone, still seething after his quarrel with Tucker.

"Noah? Maddie."

"Hey, doc." Noah let out a tired sigh.

"Honey, I need you to come to the office."

"What's wrong?"

"It's Julia."

"What happened?"

"Just get over here."

"I'm on my way."

Noah walked into Maddie's office and found Julia with her back to him and Maddie seated at her desk.

"What's going on?" he asked.

"Maddie, I can't believe you called Noah! How could you?" Julia spun around.

"*Jesus!*" Noah bristled when he saw Julia. "That bastard's a dead man."

"Noah, please just leave him alone," Julia begged. Noah took Julia's arm and pulled her over to the mirror on the wall.

"Look at yourself, Julia. *Take a good look*

at yourself! Is this the life you wanted?"

Julia was crying again and shaking her head. Noah took her hand and together they sat on the couch. His voice softer, Noah continued. "Jules, you know you could've done better than Tucker. You could've had any man in Canton. You were so beautiful and so popular. Look what he's done to you, to your life. You have to know what he is, that's he not working until two in the morning. You're smarter than that, Julia."

"I know, Noah. I'm not stupid. I'm just scared of him. I'm scared of what he'll do if I leave him. I know he doesn't love me, he loves my name...I'm just scared," Julia continued to sob. "I just can't imagine my life any other way anymore. He's all I know now."

"You don't have to be scared. You've got Mother and Dad, you've got me and Maddie. Hell, you know you've even got Julian. We're going to see you through this, okay? Now Maddie's going to fix you up and I'm going to take care of Donovan."

"What are you going to do?" Julia asked nervously.

"I'm having him arrested and I'm personally clearing all of his stuff from your house."

"*Noah!*" Julia gasped.

"Julia, you can't tell me that you still want him?"

Julia held her head high and Maddie saw in her for the first time since meeting her, the Litchfield pride shining through. "*No*, I don't want him in my house another night. You can tell him *I* said that, too."

Noah left Julia in Maddie's hands and headed back to the harbor. En route he made two phone calls on his cell. One to Julian, who knew better than to ask any questions considering it was Donovan. Julian stopped what he was doing and managed to get an arrest warrant, even three states away. And the second call was to the sheriff's office. The Litchfields had enough pull in Canton and had funded enough election campaigns for the sheriff, there was no question as to whether they'd in turn do a favor for Noah.

"Whatcha mean, I ain't going nowhere?" Tucker asked.

"Just what I said," Noah replied. "You know that saying, Tuck? What is it? 'Your ship's come in' or 'your time's up.' Nah, that isn't it, either...."

"What the *hell* are you talking about, Litchfield?"

"Oh, now I remember that saying, 'the party's over'." Just as Noah grinned, a patrol car approached the harbor and two deputies emerged. "You see those men, right there, Donovan? Well, they're here to clean up the party mess."

"Tucker Donovan?" one of the deputies asked.

"Yeah, what of it?" Tucker answered.

"Mr. Donovan, you're under arrest." The two deputies took Tucker's arms and handcuffed him.

"For what?" Tucker stammered. Noah took the warrant from one deputy and read it aloud.

"Well, according to this warrant I have here from the DA's office, it looks like two counts of assault and battery, one count of trespassing and one count of harassment."

"From who?" again Tucker was stammering.

Noah grinned. "Well, it looks like Julian Litchfield. Jules must be went and got herself a lawyer. I believe she might've told my big brother about your little misconduct at my house last night, too."

Tucker laughed out loud. "It'll never stick. She'll be bailing me out before they can get these cuffs off."

Noah shook his head. "Not this time, Tucker. Seems she's also got Julian filing separation papers as we speak. You've hit her for the last time. It stops here. 'The party's over'. You're fired, too, by the way."

"What? You can't fire me!"

"You had a job as long as you were married to my sister. As of today, that marriage is coming to an end. No marriage. *No job.*

"She ain't leaving me, Noah. She ain't got the balls...." Tucker said as the deputies lowered his head and seated him in the car.

"You're right, Donovan. She's not leaving you. *You're* leaving her. Her house, her shares, her stock. Everything's in her name, smartest thing she ever did," Noah informed Tucker.

"It'll never happen, Noah. Just wait, it'll never happen."

"Oh, it *will* happen, Donovan. She's a Litchfield, *it will happen.*"

Noah and three of his crew spent the day at Julia's, packing all of Tucker's belongings into boxes. They cleaned out the storage shed, the tool shed, loaded all of his yard equipment and boats onto trailers and hauled it all over to one of Tucker's friend's house. Julia kept a watchful eye on the goings-on, and didn't let them forget one thing.

When Noah returned later that evening, he found her still pacing, red-eyed and nervous. "Tucker's in jail and all of his stuff is at Lawton's house. If he comes back, I'll kill him. If you *let* him come back, I'll kill *you.* This crap's gone on for years and I'm sick of it."

"I know this is the right thing to do, but how am I going to start my life over now? I'm forty-five years old, what am I supposed to do?"

"Get some sleep for now. And then, we'll take it one day at a time. Mr. Charlie will here at seven in the morning to change your locks. Donovan won't make bail until after nine, so that gives Mr. Charlie a couple of hours to get that job done. In the meantime, don't take any of Tucker's calls and I'll be back in the morning to check on you. Call me if you need me?"

"I will. Noah, what happened to me?" Julia

asked as she hugged her little brother.

"Same thing that happens to a lot of us, Jules. We get so wrapped up in what we think is right for us, we don't recognize when it's wrong."

Noah had missed an entire day's work, and had kept three of his men from making any money that day. On his way to Maddie's he called the guys to let them know he was still paying them for a day's work. They'd done him a huge favor by helping out, whether on the boats or not and they would be paid for it. It was that kind of appreciation that had kept men working for the Litchfields for nearly half a century.

****

As they lay in bed that night, Maddie asked Noah, "Do you think you should have moved so fast? I mean, moving all of his things, changing the locks?"

"I had to, Doc. With Julia, you can't wait a second. Give her too much time and she'll change her mind. If she ever starts thinking about it, or Tucker has one chance to smooth things over, you can forget it."

"But you can't run her life, you can't make her divorce him if she really doesn't want to."

"No, I can't. But I can make it where she has some time to see him for what he really is. She needs some time with her old friends, some time to remember what her life was like before he screwed it up."

"I hope you're right."

****

The next few months went by slowly and Julia successfully stayed away from Tucker. She refused his calls, his messages, and after seeing the police officer parked across the street several days in a row, Tucker stopped driving by. When the divorce papers arrived, Julia signed them without looking back. She kept busy with old friends, played bridge once a week, was making new friends and was even performing with the local players' group in a rendition of 'Bye-Bye, Birdie'. At Noah's insistence, Julia had started doing the books for Litchfield and was finding her place in the world again.

CHAPTER FOURTEEN

Fall had arrived in Canton Cope and with the shrimping season and tourist season winding down, the town was again quiet and peaceful. Thanksgiving was only two weeks away and the elder Litchfields had invited Maddie and Moby to join them for the holiday dinner. Noah had practically moved in with Maddie and the townspeople had begun to call him 'Mr. Doc', which he loved.

"Christmas in Paris?" Maddie asked as she snuggled closer to Noah. The sun had been up for an hour, but it was Saturday and no reason to be in a hurry to get out of bed.

"Yeah, that's just what I said. But Mother and Dad are hell bent on going. Julia's so excited, she's about to explode," Noah smiled.

"I'm so glad they asked her along with it

being her first year without Tucker. So, what about Julian and Celeste and the kids?"

"They're going to Connecticut to be with her folks."

"And are you going?"

"They asked both of us, of course. But I knew you had your heart set on going back to Charleston so I declined."

Maddie was surprised. "Noah? You turned down Paris?"

"Doc, I'm sorry," Noah propped up on one elbow, " if I'd known you really wanted to go....it's no problem, I'll just tell them we do want to join them."

"No, no. I still want to go home, but you should go. I can't ask you to miss Christmas with your family."

"Maddie," Noah wrapped his arms around her, "I'm not spending Christmas without you. I've had 35 Christmases with my family and I'm not about to miss our first one together. I've been to Paris a few times, so I'm not missing anything there."

"You'd give up the holiday with your family, to spend it with me?" Maddie was dumbfounded.

"Doc, I love you. And wherever I am on December 25th will be a day in Paris as long as you're there with me. Got it?"

"But it's Paris, Noah..."

"Yes, it's Paris. And it will be Paris for the rest of our lives. I'll take you there myself one day, without my parents tagging along...how's that sound?"

They spent the day in and out of bed, watching old Andy Griffith reruns and making love. Nothing had ever felt so right for Maddie and Noah wouldn't have been anywhere else in the world if given the chance.

****

The first part of the week, Noah walked down to the docks to check the fax machine and make a few phone calls. Maddie was at her office, tying up some loose ends before the holidays. He was on the phone when he saw Jasper and his youngest boy, fishing from the bow of the 'Miss Isabella Maria'. Noah tapped on the window of the office and motioned for Jasper to come inside.

"Noah, how's ya been?" Jasper greeted, shaking Noah's hand.

"Hello, my friend. How's the off-season treating you?"

"Oh, fine, jis fine. Joyin' bein wid da chillen. I hare ya been holin' up wid da doc lady. I tells ya someday you's gonna scraightun up," Jasper chuckled.

"You always were right, Jasp," Noah laughed back. "I tell you man, that woman's got my heart in a vice grip. I just never imagined having this sort of feeling. I get crazy just thinking about her."

"Sounds like ya done fall and fall hard, too. Ya tole her yet?"

"Told her what?" Noah smiled at Jasper.

"Dat ya loves her, fool! Whadda hell ya thought I mean?"

"Yeah, Jasp. I've told her, about a thousand times. Seems like every time I open my mouth it's to tell her I love her."

"And her?"

Noah grinned from ear to ear. "Yes, she loves me. She loves me in ways I have never dreamed of before."

"When's ya gonna ax her?"

"Ask her what?"

"Don be gittin slow wid me, Mista Doc!" Jasper winked. "You know what I's talkin' bout."

Noah laughed. "You know me better than I know myself. I'm going over to Hilliard's today to pick out a ring. I'm going to ask her on Thanksgiving Day."

"Lawd, da heavens is rejoicin'!" Jasper jumped up. "Noah Litchfield done loss his own mind! Galdamity, boy, I's proud of ya!" He wrapped his arms around Noah in a bear hug.

"Now don't be telling everybody just yet.

Thanksgiving's still a week away and I want it to be a surprise. You can tell Sadie, but she's got to promise to keep quiet down at the Cavern."

"Oh, yessa, she be quiet! Lawd, she gonna cry her head off, she be so happy!"

****

Grace Hilliard's mouth dropped to the floor. "You what?"

"You heard me, Grace. I want a ring, specially made for Maddie," Noah said again.

"Engagement?" Grace stammered.

"Of course...are you surprised?"

"To say the least...but very happy for you. Claude will be tinkled pink. You know, we feel like you're one of our own. I imagine your parents are beside themselves with joy."

"They don't know yet, Grace. And I want to keep it that way." Noah gave Grace that look that meant he was dead serious. "I want Maddie and I to tell them together, so I'd appreciate it if you and Claude keep it quiet."

"Of course, darlin'," Grace touched Noah's cheek with her wrinkled hand. "We'll not breathe it. Now what do you want to look at first?"

"I want to see your gems, no settings. I want Claude to design a one-of-a-kind band; I want something like nothing else in this world."

Money was no question and Noah spent very little time making his decision. He knew the stones he wanted the moment he saw them. He chose a 3-carat emerald-cut pale emerald, the color of Maddie's eyes. To accompany it, he choose two diamond baguettes, each a carat, to adorn either side of the emerald. Claude came in as Noah was making his choices and grinned a country mile when Grace told him Noah's news.

"Claude, I want a one-of-a-kind band for these babies. White gold. Maybe something with some filigree. I want it to look like it's from another time, another century. Maddie's big on antebellum stuff and I think she'd love something that looked like it was from another era. Can you do that?"

"Absolutely, Noah. That won't be a problem," Claude replied. "Shall I go ahead and make wedding bands, as well?"

Noah smiled. "Absolutely. Hopefully, I'll be back for those."

"How soon do you need this done?" Claude asked.

"The day before Thanksgiving. Will that be a problem?"

"That's not a problem. The tourist season is over and the holiday is still a week and a couple of days away. I can get it done for you." Claude confirmed.

"That's good. That's real good." Noah was pleased.

****

Maddie was peeling potatoes when Noah came in.

"Hey there, doc. What smells so good?" he asked as he kissed her neck.

"Roast beef. Want to grate those carrots for me?" she smiled back.

"Sure thing. How was your day?" Noah asked as he began to wash the carrots.

"Quiet. The flu doesn't seem to have hit too many people yet. How about you?"

"The same. Went to the office this morning and had a nice visit with Jasper. He and Cedric were fishing, looked like they did pretty good, too. I worry about him during the off-season."

"Why is that?"

"Money gets pretty tight for them when we're not working. And that shack they live in doesn't even have air conditioning, great heat, but no air."

"I thought the guys made good money...."

"They do, we pay them top dollar. The rest of the crew does fine, but Jasp and Sadie have six kids and they've put them all through college. When Ced finishes high school, they'll send him, too. They've all gotten some grants, I'm sure Cedric will too, but other than that, no kind of help."

"They're proud people, Noah, and I think they should be commended for wanting their children to be educated."

"Yeah, I know. I just wish Jasper would let me find them a little house somewhere that was livable. He won't even talk about it. He's too proud."

Maddie turned from the stove and put her arms around Noah. "Noah Litchfield, I love you. Every day I love you more. Your heart is so full and you truly care about those guys at the docks. I wonder if they know how lucky they are to work with you."

Noah wrapped his arms around Maddie and pulled her closer. "I think it's the other way around. I have to keep reminding myself how lucky I am to be working with them. They've been a part of my family for years and I can't imagine working with a better group of guys."

Maddie softly kissed Noah on the lips. “I would never have believed nine months ago that I would have known you so well, or loved you so much this very day.”

“Sometimes I can’t believe it either. I’m actually holding you in my arms and never wanting to let go.”

Noah kissed her again and she responded by kissing him a little harder. He reached down and pulled her hips tightly to his as Maddie ran her hand down his back and pulled his buttocks towards her. In one quick move they were on the kitchen floor. In seconds, they were free of their clothes and completely absorbed in each other.

Noah wasted no time in taking her, filling her with his manhood, as Maddie eagerly raised her hips to meet him. It was over as quickly as it had begun and they both laughed at the suddenness of their passion.

As they lay on the floor, giggling like teenagers, they heard Julia call out to them from the back door. As they scrambled to get dressed, Maddie called out to her to come on in. Their flushed faces and rapid breathing told Julia she had interrupted playtime.

"You two rabbits at it again, huh?" Julia laughed.

"Julia......" Noah was embarrassed.

"Oh, don't 'Julia' me, little brother. I wasn't born yesterday. And I don't blame you one bit."

"Hey, Jules," Maddie hugged Julia. "How ya been?"

"Great. I thought I'd come by and see ya'll. It's been a while."

"You want to stay for supper?" Noah invited.

"Please do stay," Maddie blushed. "It's not quite ready yet. We....uh, got a little side-tracked, but it shouldn't be too long."

"Oh, why not? What can I do to help?"

An hour or so later, they were sitting around the dinner table, stomachs full. Since Julia's divorce from Tucker she had become a new person. She was a delight to be around and had become one of Maddie's closest friends in the Cope. Noah was happy to have his sister back, back to being the person he once knew her to be.

"I got a letter from Tucker today." Julia said sarcastically.

"Really.....what's the ass-wipe up to these days?" Noah snickered.

“He wanted to let me know he’s living in Kentucky now. Getting married, too.” Julia said.

“Married?” Maddie exclaimed.

“To who? Someone in Kentucky? A relative no doubt.....” Noah joked.

Julia laughed. “He actually wanted to give me another chance to ask him to come back, can you believe that? Like I’d even look his way again. I’ve come too far and gotten my life back together. There’s not a chance in hell.”

“Boy, I’m glad to hear you talking like that, Jules,” Noah sighed. “I can’t tell you how it hurt me to see you with him.”

“Oh, Noah,” Julia leaned over and kissed her brother on the cheek. “I’m sorry. I was just so young when I met him, and so blind.”

“Well, you’re moving on with your life, “ Maddie added, “and that’s what’s important. And from what your mother tells me, you've met someone."

"What is this?" Noah questioned, smiling at his sister.

Julia grinned. "Well, not exactly. I've known him all my life, but he's just moved back to the Cope."

"You're not talking about Hamp?" Noah asked.

"Hamp? Who is he?" Maddie was curious now.

"Yes, Noah. It's Hamp." Julia turned to Maddie. "Hampton Limehouse. We dated in high school and I absolutely adored him. But he enlisted in the Navy right after graduation and well, I met Tucker and the rest is history."

"Oh, that's wonderful!" Maddie exclaimed.

"How did he come to be back here?"

"He just retired from the military and has come home to open an antiques store."

"Is he divorced or what?" Noah asked.

"Widowed. His wife passed away three years ago. Cancer."

"How sad....but wow....how great that he's come back here. To find you." Maddie gushed.

"Maddie, now, don't go rushing into things. We're just dating and getting to know each other again. I'm taking things slow."

"Well, one thing's for sure, " Noah stated, "Hampton definitely comes from better stock than Tucker. Thank god."

****

Maddie's ring was ready the Wednesday before Thanksgiving and Noah made special plans with Simon to have lunch reservations for himself and Maddie. Moby wasn't due at the Cope until around 3:00 the day of Thanksgiving, so Noah made his plans to ask Maddie to marry him at The Veranda.

Simon had arranged for them to have lunch on the Laurel Lanai where they'd had their first date. The holidays were always a very busy time for Simon, but he took special measures to accommodate Noah's request. They would have the Lanai to themselves; no other reservations were made for that area. Noah was a nervous wreck and hoped Maddie couldn't tell. As far as Maddie knew, he was just Noah. She had no idea what he was up to. They enjoyed a quiet lunch and tried to leave room for the colossal dinner Jestine was preparing for that evening.

"I'm kind of surprised Simon isn't busier today, with it being a holiday and all. I'd assumed these tables would have been filled completely." Maddie queried.

Noah smiled. "Well, Simon knows his stuff and I can assure you he's lost no money today on empty tables. He did this just for us, Maddie. "

"He what?" Maddie grinned back.

"I wanted us to be completely alone today. We're going to be surrounded by my entire family tonight and I wanted this afternoon to be special, just us."

"You never cease to surprise me...."

"I hope you always feel that way." Noah stood and took Maddie's hand. "Let's go for a walk."

They walked down to the lawn and strolled beneath the magnolias and live oaks. It was a cool afternoon, not quite cold yet. Canton wouldn't see a hard freeze until late January or early February.

They descended the ancient steps leading to the shore from the property and walked in the surf, hand in hand. The tide was coming in, but the Atlantic was giving them all the walking room they needed.

“I love you, doc.” Noah whispered as he lightly kissed her cheek.

“I love you, too,” Maddie whispered back, as they continued to walk.

Noah smiled. “I hope you know how much you’ve changed me in this last year. I’m not the same person I was before you moved here.”

“Noah, I haven’t changed you. You’ve done that on your own. People reach a point in their lives when they realize it’s time to become established. To get their lives grounded with both feet firmly planted. I had no part in that for you, you came to that place on your own.”

"Maddie, I love you and I want you to be with me for the rest of my life. I've never loved anyone before you and I never will ever again. This is it for me. My heart aches when you're not by my side and I don't want to think about you not ever being there."

"Noah?" Maddie was worried. "Where is all of this coming from? What's wrong?"

Noah stopped walking and turned Maddie to face him. He dropped to one knee and reached into his breast pocket. In his hand he held a black velvet box. Maddie gasped and her heart was pounding so loudly she was sure those still eating at The Veranda could hear it.

"Doc, I love you, " Noah said yet again, as he opened the box and took the ring from its resting place. "Will you say yes and spend the rest of your life with me? Will you marry me?"

His hand trembled as he slipped the

perfectly sized ring on Maddie's finger. Maddie's hands were shaking as badly as his and tears ran down her face.

"Yes." she whispered so softly Noah wasn't sure he had heard her.

"Yes?" he smiled, lifting her chin so that he could see her eyes.

"Yes!" Maddie exclaimed. Noah wrapped her in his arms and lifted her up into his embrace.

They returned arm in arm, to The Veranda and drove slowly to the ferry. The trip home was full of talk of the future and how happy they would be. How happy the Litchfields would be and how sad it was that Maddie's parents weren't here to share in their happiness. They were both still floating when they arrived at Noah's house. They chose to go to Noah's because Moby would be arriving at Maddie's in a few hours and they didn't want to be interrupted for awhile. Noah began undressing Maddie the minute she stepped from his BMW and she followed suit, slowly, seductively, unzipping his trousers and running her hands under his shirt and up his chest. They kissed softly, then they kissed fiercely, as they stumbled in the front door and found their way to Noah's bed.

The windows were open and the gentle ocean breeze blew through the curtains and kissed their naked bodies as they made love. They had never before made love so quietly, so softly and without a word spoken between them. No words were needed, their bodies and their eyes spoke all there was to say.

The only sounds to be heard were the seagulls on the beach, the roar of the tide as it made its way back to the shore and the gentle sighs and moans as Noah and Maddie both came together in hushed shudders. The covers were strewn from the bed, the pillows were lost to the hardwood floor and the only thing between the two of them was their collective sweat.

"I can't believe we're getting married," Maddie whispered.

"I can't believe you're marrying *me*," Noah replied with a grin. Noah caressed her arm and ran one finger across her breast. "What did I ever do before you moved here?"

"I'm not sure. I'm not sure I ever *lived* before I moved here."

"Do you think you can live with me for the next fifty years?"

"I know one thing. I can't imagine living *without* you for the next fifty years."

From the comfort of the bed and each other's arms, they heard the muffled jingle of Maddie's cell phone which was in her purse, on the floor in the kitchen. Noah looked at Maddie. Maddie looked at Noah.

"Do we have to answer it?" he asked, jokingly. Maddie glanced at the clock beside the bed.

"Ugh, it's after three. I bet it's Moby." Noah rose from the bed and ran to get the phone.

"Hiya, " he said, after recognizing Moby's number on the phone screen.

"Hiya yourself. Where the hell are ya'll?" Moby laughed. "Some welcome party I got."

"Uhh, sorry 'bout that, Moby. We're over at my house." Noah laughed.

"What the hell are y'all doing over there? Never mind, I *know* what ya'll are doing over there."

"Hold on, " Noah laughed again. "Here's

the doc." He handed Maddie the phone and curled up beside her again.

"Hey you," Maddie said into the phone.

"Hey *you*. Having fun?" Moby joked.

"Well, as a matter of fact...." Maddie giggled, as she climbed on top of Noah. "Yeah, I'm having a damn good time."

"Geez....can't ya'll give it a rest? You've got company over here. Hungry company on top of that."

"I know, I know. I've kind of worked up a little appetite myself."

"TMI, girlfriend. TMI. Can I just let myself in?" Moby asked.

"Yep. By all means. Still got your key?" Maddie replied.

"Sure do. When can I expect you two lovebirds to join me?" Moby laughed again.

"Five minutes. Just let us get dressed." Maddie answered, only to have Noah take the phone from her and say, "fifteen minutes, maybe twenty. That work for you, kiddo?"

"Do I have a choice?" Moby asked, laughing.

"Ummm, no, not this time, " Noah laughed.

"Didn't think so. I'll see ya'll when you get here. And listen, while you're getting some, how 'bout tell Maddie to get some for me, too. Okay?"

"Will do, babe. See ya shortly." Noah closed the phone and tossed it onto the covers on the floor. "Moby says to get some for her while you're getting....." he smiled at Maddie.

"Did she now?" Maddie asked, reaching down to caress Noah between his legs. "Well, let's not disappoint her."

"By all means, doc, let's not......"

****

The newly engaged couple arrived at Maddie's with just enough time to shower and get ready for the holiday dinner at Noah's parents' home. Moby had taken advantage of the time waiting for them to get home by showering and getting herself ready. She was dressed and tapping her foot when they walked in the door.

"Well, it's about time," she smiled at them. "You know they make a pill or something you can take to control those kind of urges....you're a doctor, you should know that...."

Maddie ran up to her and gave her a big hug. "I'm so glad you're here! I'm so sorry we weren't home when you got in."

"Oh, it's okay. I just love giving you a hard time, " she hugged Maddie back and turned to hug Noah. "And apparently, so does Noah...." They all laughed out loud. Moby was such a character and never bit her tongue. She said *exactly* what she was thinking, when she was thinking it and didn't care who she offended in the process. It was one of the main reasons Maddie loved her so much....she could always let whoever have it when they needed to get it. Maddie was so eager to tell Moby their news and Noah had told her on the drive home that it was okay to tell her. She thought Moby deserved to hear it first, before anyone else. Moby was a sister to Maddie in all ways but biological, and she wanted to let Moby be the first one she told. However, Moby having the eagle-eye that she had, noticed the ring right away.

"What the H is that?" she exclaimed, grabbing Maddie's hand.

"That would be an *engagement ring!*"

Maddie glowed.

"Oh my god....you son-of-a-bitch....you asked her to marry you, didn't you?" She punched Noah in the arm. Noah laughed.

"Yes, I did, Moby and she said yes."

"Well, of course, she said yes. I'd have had to kill her if she'd said no."

"Of course I said yes. I love this man completely...." Maddie replied, putting her arm around Noah's waist.

"Oh god, this is wonderful. Now I get to plan a wedding...have you set a date yet?" Moby asked.

"No, not yet. In fact, we haven't even talked about that part yet." Noah replied.

"No, you've been too busy consummating a

marriage that hasn't even happened yet. Boy, ya'll need to get your priorities in order." Moby joked.

Thanksgiving dinner came and went and the Litchfield family gathered in the living room to let their meal settle and to visit. Julia had brought along Hampton and Maddie thought he was surely the best looking man in the Cope, next to Noah, of course. And he was obviously very happy to be seeing Julia again.

Julian, Celeste and their two children, Kirk and Mary Grace, had flown in from D.C. for the holiday. It was the first time Maddie had met them and she found Julian to be a clone of Noah, only older. The family resemblance was strong. Celeste was polite at best, very *persnippity* as Moby would have said. The children on the other hand were extremely warm and carefree and so happy to see their Uncle Noah. Kirk at 13 and Mary Grace at 11, were still too young to be snobs. And beautiful, simply beautiful. They both had inherited the

Litchfield love of the sea and had made Noah promise that after dinner, he'd take them for a sailboat ride around the harbor.

Noah cleared his throat, took Maddie by the hand, and they stood from their seat on the sofa."Everyone, if I could change the subject for just a minute, please..." he started.

All eyes were on them as Noah continued."You all know that Maddie and I have been seeing each other for almost a year now. I don't know when or how I knew, but it was early in our relationship that I knew I didn't want to ever be without her."

Kirkland smiled at his son and Jestine nodded with approval."Well, long story short, I've asked her to marry me, just this afternoon in fact, and she's said yes. So...."

The family all cheered and cried. Julia was

sobbing with joy and Jestine couldn't stop hugging Maddie and Noah.

Kirkland shook his son's hand and gave him a big hug. "I'm so proud of you, son, and even more happy for you."

Julian hugged his brother and congratulated him."Noah, she's quite a catch and I'm very proud of you." Julian said. He then hugged Maddie and welcomed her to the family. "You know, Maddie, he is a great guy. It's just took him some time to realize that."

Celeste gave Maddie and Noah both a very royal hug, lukewarm at best, and wished them the best. "This family has always made me feel welcome and wanted, and I've always known that I could come to them for anything. I'm sure they've welcomed you the same way. I will be extremely proud to be your sister-in-law." It surprised both Maddie and Noah that Celeste would say something so kind after being so standoffish, and it made them both very happy.

The children were elated to say the least. "Can we call you Aunt Maddie now, or do we have to wait until you're married?" Mary Grace wanted to know.

"I'd love it if you called me Aunt Maddie, *right now,*" Maddie hugged them.

Sweet Dreams, Doc

CHAPTER FIFTEEN

Christmas was fast approaching. Maddie and Noah had decorated a tree at Maddie's and opted to not do much at Noah's as he was hardly there anymore. The tree was beautiful as was the cedar hanging from the porch banisters and red bows adorning it. The Litchfields, along with Julia and Hamp left for Paris the week before Christmas and Maddie was planning their trip to Charleston. They both agreed to leave a few days before the holiday to beat traffic and have a few extra days in the Holy City to enjoy.

The night before they were to leave, their bags packed, they lay in bed talking about the future.

"Have you thought anymore about a date?" Maddie asked.

"Yeah, I was thinking tomorrow would be a

good day, " Noah smiled at her.

"Yeah, it would. But I don't think anyone would forgive us if we did that with almost everyone we love out of the country."

"Nah, I don't think that's such a good idea."

"So...how about the fall?" Maddie suggested.

"The fall? That's so far away. I want to hurry up and make a decent woman out of you," Noah laughed, kissing Maddie on her neck, making her giggle.

"But it will be cooler. And I was thinking of having something outdoors. It would be so much nicer if it was cooler. Don't you think?"

"Yeah, I think it would be much nicer. But where were you thinking?"

"I don't know. I think the right thing would

be to get married in our church, don't you?"

"Well, yeah. But what about The Veranda?" Noah thought.

"Oh, gosh, that would be beautiful, wouldn't it? I'd never thought of that. But what would your folks say about us not getting married in the church?"

Noah thought about that for a second. "Well, I don't think they'd approve, actually. But...it is our wedding, you know. And they wouldn't deny us that, but I don't think they'd be pleased. No."

"Okay, what about this then. What if we get married in the church and have the reception at Simon's place? How about that?" Maddie's eyes lit up at the thought and Noah couldn't help but smile realizing how happy that idea made her.

"I think you've got something there. I think it would be perfect."

****

They arrived in Charleston four days before Christmas, checked into their suite at the Lodge Alley Inn and before they could even think about it, had made love in the king size bed, with the French doors open to the street below. It was a comfortable sixty degrees outside and the Lowcountry breeze was just enough that they snuggled deep under one blanket.

They spent the extra days touring the city, Maddie showing Noah all of the historical landmarks she'd grown up around. The Battery, Rainbow Row, The Citadel, Fort Sumter, the Market and all the fine dining on Market and East Bay Streets. They shopped on King Street and took a carriage tour of the downtown area.

They spent Christmas Eve with Moby and

her new beau, Clint DiMare. Clint was the director of operations for the local minor league baseball team and a handsome man. He fit well with Moby and she was unbelievably happy.

Christmas morning, Maddie and Noah drove to the cemetery to see Maddie's parents. She had brought poinsettias for their graves and Noah couldn't help but get tears in his eyes when Maddie introduced them to him. He hugged her close and cried with her when he realized just how much she missed her parents, especially her mother.

Now more than ever, with a wedding around the corner, he knew how much she needed her mom. They then drove to Maddie's home to show Noah where she had grown up and then out to look at the property left to her by her parents.

"I don't know what I'll do with this land, but I couldn't sell it." Maddie confessed.

"Well, maybe one day, we'll build a vacation home here. How's that sound?" Noah suggested.

"A vacation home? In my hometown?"

"Well, maybe not a vacation home, just a *second* home. How's that sound?"

"That sounds wonderful. We could spend some of the off-season here, weekends anyway, when I won't be needed at the office. Holidays. *Vacations*," Maddie rolled her eyes up at Noah.

"See? That's what I'm talking about. You know we already have two homes now...I don't know what I'm going to do with mine."

"Well, let's sell mine. You've had yours longer, it means so much to you, I don't think we should sell it."

Noah shook his head. "No, I kind of like the thought of living closer to the harbor, to the docks.

You know, where I'm needed. My place is just a bachelor's place, not very inviting."

"It could be inviting if the right woman was given the chance to make it a real home."

Noah's eyes lit up. "Doc, you just gave me a great idea! What if I gave my place to Jasper and Sadie?"

"Noah, do you think they'd take it? I mean, they're so proud and they don't like handouts."

"If I make it seem like he's doing a favor for me, taking care of the place, while I don't use it, he'll take it in a heartbeat."

Three days after Christmas they returned home, tired and weary, but loving every second of the trip. The Litchfields weren't due back until after the new year, so things were fairly quiet and relaxed.

Sweet Dreams, Doc

CHAPTER SIXTEEN

One morning not long after returning from Charleston, Noah woke up before the sun rose and walked down to the office. There were a few faxes to tend to and some messages on the machine, but nothing that couldn't wait until the next day.

He started the coffee pot in the back room and stretched out in the desk chair, legs crossed on top the desk. The sun was just starting to peak over the ocean, it was looking to be a beautiful day. Noah had just fixed a cup of coffee and walked out on the dock to watch that sun make its way on up when Sumpter walked up.

"Hey der, brotha Noah...", Sumpter greeted.

"Well, hey there yourself, Mr. Antley. How the hell are you?" Noah shook hands with him.

"Jis great...lovin' life, man, lovin' life."

Sweet Dreams, Doc

"You just can't stay away from this dock, can you, man?" Noah laughed.

"No suh, show can't. Looks lak ya can't neivah."

"No sir, sure can't." Noah quoted Sumpter.

"I hare say ya gittin' married?"

"That would be correct, my brother. That I am."

"Well, I thank dat's 'bout da bes news I hared in a long time. Ya happy, ain't ya?"

"Absolutely. Never happier. It's almost like a dream, you know?"

"I show do. My Tisha, lawd, I don know what I do widout her. Dat's my life right dare, you know, man? It's all 'bout dat. What ya got in hare..." Sumpter pointed to his heart.

"No truer words ever spoken, my friend.

It's all about what's in your heart."

"Look hare, let me tells ya while I down hare. I be heard dat Wells gal, what's her name?"

Noah's face went ashen. He hadn't thought of her in over a year. "Melissa."

"Yeah, Melissa, dat's it. I be heard she had died, man. Ya heard 'bout dat, Noah?" Sumpter asked.

"Jesus....no. I haven't heard that. What happened?" Noah was shocked.

"Da big C, man, cancer. Took her quick lak, too."

"God. Was she here, in the Cope?"

"No man, she had moved on up north somewheres. Say she ain't had no family or nuttin."

"No, she had no family. That I knew of. She was in foster care for a long time, years I think, before she ever moved here. Man, that girl had a lot of problems. I sure hate to hear that," Noah was saddened at the thought of Melissa being sick, dying even, with no one or no family to surround her. "What was she doing up north?"

"I ain't know, man. She lef hare not long afta ya start seeing da doc." Noah tried to remember if he had even told Melissa that he was moving on, seeing someone else. To his embarrassment, she was never more than a tool he used to make Maddie jealous. Which hadn't worked in the first place, but he hated himself for using Melissa that way.

"So when did she die? Where is she buried?" Noah asked.

"She had died a coupla weeks fo Chrimas. She buried up in Jersey, I thank."

"Jersey? What the hell was she doing way the hell up there?"

"I ain't know, man. Dat's all I's got. She dead. She be in da ground up in Jersey somewheres. Jis thought ya'd wanna know'd 'bout it."

"Yeah, I'd want to know about it. Thanks, Sumpter. I appreciate you telling me. I just wish I had a way of getting in touch with whoever buried her, whoever was responsible for her in the end. I'd like to pay my respects."

"Well, ya's might wanna check wid dat gal she be hangin' round when she was here. Dat 'ole Simmons gal. One dat work up dere wid Sadie. She might know."

"I might just do that, Sumpter," Noah said.

****

Sweet Dreams, Doc

Noah walked back up to the house to find Maddie still in bed. It was only a little after 7 a.m. and he wasn't ready to wake her just yet. She didn't have to be at the office until nearly nine, he'd let her sleep for a while. He slipped his flip-flops offs, along with his jeans, and slid back into bed. He curled up beside Maddie and took her in his arms. She moaned softly and snuggled deep into arms without waking. How could he tell her about Melissa? It wasn't like this girl had been his girlfriend or anything, but he had dated her a few times, slept with her even. Learning now of her death, he was ridden with guilt for using this woman. There was no emotional attachment or detachment for that matter, but he felt guilty nonetheless. Melissa was so young and so full of life. To have it all end so soon didn't seem fair. And to have no one there when she was sick, no one to look after her, to care for her, or even care once she was gone, was just more than he could imagine.

Maddie opened her eyes to find Noah in deep thought, a million miles away. He looked worried, distraught even and she immediately knew something was wrong. "Hey you...what's wrong?" she asked.

"Morning, doc," Noah leaned over and kissed her good morning.

"What's the matter? I can tell something's wrong. What is it?"

"I walked down to the docks this morning and met up with Sumpter. He gave me some news that's kind of set me back a bit." Maddie sat up in bed, glanced at the clock, which blinked only 7:30 so she had some time before needing a shower. "What news, Noah?"

"Well, this girl that I use to mess around with some, before you and me, I mean....she moved away from here last year, according to Sumpter, I didn't even know she had left town."

"And? What about this girl?"

"She died, Maddie. She had cancer and she died."

"Oh my god, how awful. How old was she?"

Noah sighed. "I'm not really even sure. I think she was close to thirty maybe, thirty-one. I just can't believe she died."

"Well, honey, it's terrible, but it happens to so many people. Cancer is not prejudice, that's for sure."

"I know. I know all that. But she had no one. No family. No friends that could've or would've, taken care of her. Nothing. Nobody. She just got sick, suffered and died. Alone."

Maddie put her arms around Noah. "It's

okay, baby. It's okay. But you can't beat yourself up because you weren't there for her. You didn't know. How could you have known if she wasn't even living here any longer?"

"I don't know. I'm just feeling so guilty for treating her the way I did," he looked at Maddie. "I'm ashamed to admit this, but I only used her to make you jealous. I know it didn't work, but that's all it was, I used her outright. And when I was done with her, I just tossed her to the side. Like a piece of garbage. I knew she had no family. No friends worth knowing. I knew all of that and still, I just walked away. I tried to remember this morning if I even told her that I was moving on, that I didn't want to see her anymore. I honestly can't remember the last conversation we had."

Maddie remembered her visit from Jasper over a year ago. He had told her that Noah was trying to make her jealous, but she kept her word and didn't mention it to Noah. "Noah, it's okay. I kind of figured that's what you were doing and it doesn't matter now, none of that matters. If she left town, it wasn't because of you. You have to believe that. If she had such a rough life, as you say she's had, leaving town was what she did best probably. New town, new faces, change of scenery, that sort of thing. Maybe she thought she could start over somewhere else. Who knows? But you can't make yourself sick worrying over what you said to her the last time you saw her."

Noah shook his head in agreement, if only slight agreement. "I know. It's not like we were an item. We only went out a few times...", he looked at Maddie, "but you need to know this...I did sleep with her. I did and I regret now, but I did and I'm sorry."

Maddie laughed. "Noah, I know you slept with her. You've slept with half the available women in this town. You think I don't know that?"

He smiled. "Yeah, I guess you pretty much figured that out already, huh?"

"Yeah, I figured that out already. I also knew you were disease free long before I ever went out with you, too," Maddie confessed.

"Well, just how the hell did you know that?," Noah laughed.

Maddie giggled a little. "That night you cut your hand on the oyster knife."

"Yeah, what about it?"

"Well, I took a little extra time numbing you up. Made sure you wouldn't feel anything. Drew some blood while you weren't looking...which by the way was the entire time, you're such a wuss...and had it tested." She smiled at him sheepishly.

"You did what?" Noah laughed out loud.

"Isn't that a direct violation of some Hippocratic oath, or OSHA or HIPAA or some shit like that? Don't I need to sign some kind of consent form before I'm tested for anything?"

"Yep, you're right on all accounts. But what are you going to do about now? Huh? Once I got the clear card on you, I knew you were healthy at least. I wasn't about to go out with you without knowing what might jump off of you and jump on me." Maddie grinned.

"So tell me..." Noah said as he gently pushed her back onto the bed and straddled her. "What else did you do to me while I was sedated? Any other stories you care to share with me?"

"No other stories, my dear, " she leaned up from the bed and kissed him, "as of yet. Who knows what the future may bring though..."

"You scare me, you know that. Now I'm going to have to watch my back with you all the time."

Maddie pushed Noah from atop her. "Get off me now, I gotta go to work. I don't have time to play with you anymore, so mind your manners or I'm bringing a syringe home from work." She grinned at him as she got out of bed. She ran her hands through his hair and kissed him gently. "Are you going to be okay?"

He smiled up at her. "Yeah, I'm going to be fine. I'll shake this in a few hours, get it off my mind. It'll be okay. If it's okay with you though, I'd like to try and find out where she's buried, or who took care of everything, just to pay my respects. You know? I didn't respect her much when she was alive, it's the least I can do now. What do you think?"

"I think that's exactly what you should do. You wouldn't be much of a man if you didn't. And

I know you, if you don't do this, it'll tear you up inside."

"Yeah." Noah just shook his head.

****

The next day, Noah decided to pay a visit to Jasper and Sadie. He'd decided to go on and ask them about his house. The off-season was the perfect time for them to move, Jasper would have plenty of time to get settled in and comfortable. As he pulled his Wrangler in their drive, he saw Jasper sitting on the front porch, repairing a fishing net. Jasper was grinning wide when Noah stepped from the jeep.

"Hey dare, boss man! How ya doin'?" Jasper called out. Noah walked up the steps, patted Jasper on the back and joined him on the porch floor.

"Doing good, Jasp. How's everybody?"

"We's doin' good, too. Whas dis I hare 'bout ya gittin' hitched? Yo ass ain't eben come up to dis hare house and axed me nor Sadie if ya could be gittin' married and shit." Jasper was smiling.

"Man, I'm sorry about that. Is it okay with y'all if I marry Maddie?" Noah laughed.

"Show boy, damn ya knowd it's jis A-okay wid us. Sadie so damn happy, she be tellin' everbody dat her white boy gonna git married."

Noah popped Jasper on the knee. "Well, old man, I figured she'd be pretty damn happy about it. Figured as much."

"Yeah, lawd, she done be talkin' to ya moma, figurin' out what she gonna be cookin', all that stuff. Ya lak her own youngun', you know? She done went an' got all fool 'bout doin' stuff for ya. Be honest wid ya, she 'bout drive me crazy. If she like dis now, what da hell it gonna be when one a dem six a ours go and do it? Lawd amighty....I ain't know, " Jasper grinned and shook his head.

"I got a favor to ask you, Jasper," Noah started, changing the subject. "It's real important to me and you're just the person for the job."

"Was dat, boss? Ya knowd I do anythang fer ya."

"Well, with Maddie and me getting married, we're going to be sharing one house. Maddie's house. Which means mine is going to be empty. Now I don't want to sell my house to just anybody. Can't imagine some Yankee coming down here and living in my house. I was wondering if you and Sadie and the kids wouldn't mind living there for me. You know, so as to keep it up and stuff. You know an empty house don't stand long." Noah was doing his best to make this offer sound like a favor.

Jasper sat there for awhile, never stopped stitching on that net, and eventually looked at Noah. "Noah, ya knows I ain't got no money be buyin' ya house. I's got all dem chillen in college and all."

"Jasper, I'm not asking you to buy my house. I'm asking you to live there. Be the caretaker. You know, look out for the place."

"Boy, ya ain't be tryin' to gib me ya house, now is ya? Cuz ya know I ain't take no handouts from nobody....not eben ya."

Noah shook his head. "No sir. Not trying to *give* you my house. Not trying to *sell* you my house. I simply need someone to live there and take care of it for me. It's not going to keep itself and those walls need life breathing in them." Jasper didn't answer right away. "And besides, it's bigger than this house, there would be more room for all of you. It's got a great A/C unit, freeze- your-ass- off-cold, a nice big kitchen for Sadie, the kids would only have to sleep two or three to a bedroom, plus it's on the water, Jasper. No more driving to the dock to go fishing with the boys. Just walk out your back door."

"Dat sound lak a dream, boy. But I can't 'ford the utility on sometin' lak dat house. I jis don thank I da man for dat job, boss man."

"Jasper, follow me here. Since I wouldn't be selling the house or giving you the house, I'd still be paying the light bill, the phone bill, the insurance, all that stuff. All you'd have to do is *live* in it. That's it."

"Why I wanna lib in a house you pay all da bills fer? Dat ain't right. Me and dat family a mine liben up in ya house, and ya payin' all da bills. Dat ain't right!"

"Jasper you'd be taking care of the house for me. Mowing the lawn. Weeding the flower beds. Repairing the roof. Cleaning out the gutters. Trimming the hedges. Painting the shutters when they need it. That kind of stuff. It wouldn't be like you were there living free of charge. You keep up the house for me, I let you live in the house. Even trade. What do you say? You're the only man I'd ask to do this, cause you're the only man I trust enough to take care of my house."

"Well, what in sam hell is I spose to do wid mine?" Jasper asked.

"Well, now I've thought about that, too. You know from time to time, we have people come in with that contracting crew. Doing work up the road there in Georgetown. They pay pretty hefty rates to stay in those hotels. I'd bet they'd much rather pay rent to live in a house. Especially one that's in such good shape as yours. We could put a window unit in that kitchen window there and maybe one in the back, near the bedrooms, cool that house right down. They'd love staying here. It would be more like home to them."

Jasper stitched away and kept quiet. Noah didn't know if he was thinking of a way to turn Noah's offer down or a way to accept the offer without thinking it was a handout. Jasper finally stood and said to Noah, "I's gonna run dis hare by Sadie. See what she say. Come on in hare and git yoself somein' to drink." They walked in the house and after Jasper told Sadie what Noah had asked them to do, Noah had to explain it all over again to both of them. He was bound and determined not to make it sound like charity, but as a favor to him. He knew both of them would go to hell and back for him if he needed them to and he was praying that this offer sounded like a huge favor.

"Noah, sugah, dare ain't nobody ya thank would do dis fer ya but us?" Sadie asked.

"No, m'am. I'm sure of it. I don't trust anyone in this world more than ya'll and my family. I can't ask anyone in my family to do it for me, so that just leaves ya'll." Noah claimed.

"Well, Jaspa, it sound lak da me, we be gittin' ready to move on up da road. Dis hare boy need us and we's gotta hep him out," Sadie smiled.

"Well, yessir, ya heard da woman. We be movin' on up da road dare," Jasper grinned.

Sweet Dreams, Doc

CHAPTER SEVENTEEN

The New Year came in with a bang, quite literally. The Veranda has been the host sight for the annual New Year's Eve Ball since Simon bought the place and Noah and Maddie attended the celebration. It was a black tie affair and they both looked as beautiful as any couple in a magazine.

The fireworks display was set up on the shore down from the restaurant and it was spectacular. After spending the last few days helping Jasper and Sadie pack up the last 40 years of their lives and move them across town to Noah's house, the night was a welcome reprieve. They were close to being done and Sadie was as excited as a child at Christmas. She had insisted on Maddie and Noah joining them for New Year's dinner at their new home and they had gladly accepted. Sadie was promising hopping john and collards, and both of them knew it would be a fantastic meal.

The elder Litchfields, along with Julia and Hampton, had returned from Paris, full of gifts, photos and stories. It was good to have them back home, Maddie had missed them all, but especially Julia. She had grown close to Julia in the last few months and next to Moby, Maddie considered Julia her best friend. Maddie and Noah had set their wedding date for mid-October and plans were well under way. It would be the grandest wedding the Cope had seen for some time.

****

Noah had put off going to see Kat Simmons for a couple of weeks. He wasn't sure what to expect when he asked her about Melissa Wells, but he knew he'd never have any peace until he did. Something was telling him he needed to make sure she was well cared for in the end and that everything possible had been done for her. He walked into the Canton Café mid-morning, after the morning crowd and avoiding the lunchtime rush.

Kat was filling salt and pepper shakers when he walked in. She looked up when the bell above the door jingled and only nodded hello in Noah's direction. Noah pulled a stool up at the bar and whistled a cat-call to Sadie, who was busy pulling fresh poached chicken from the bone. She was getting her famous chicken salad ready for the craving patrons at lunchtime.

"Hey dare, sugah!," Sadie called out to Noah.

"Hello Sadie! How's it going?" Noah called back.

"Jis great, darlin. The lawd is good, ya know?"

"Yes, m'am, He is."

Kat walked over to the counter and poured Noah a cup of steaming coffee. She wouldn't make eye contact with Noah and he wasn't expecting a pleasant conversation from her.

"Morning, Kat," he said politely.

"Mornin'," she replied cautiously.

"You've been doing okay?"

"Like you would care one way or the other," she replied sarcastically.

Noah frowned. "Look. I know I'm your least favorite person in this town, but don't make me a brute."

"Well," Kat smiled a little, "I wouldn't say you were my *least* favorite person, but you're on my top ten list."

Noah smiled back. "That makes me feel better."

"That wasn't my intention."

"Ha, ha," Noah said. "Now that we've gotten the pleasantries out of the way, I need to talk to you for a few minutes if you're not real busy."

Kat looked at the clock on the wall which read just a little after ten. "Lunch crowd won't start coming in until around 11 or a little after. You help me fill these shakers while we talk?"

They walked over to the booth where she was working on the shakers when Noah came in and they sat down and starting pouring salt and pepper into each one. "So what's on your mind, Noah?"

"Well, I just heard a few weeks ago about Melissa." Noah couldn't help but notice the look on Kat's face. He wasn't positive, but he thought he saw a look of surprise. "You didn't know, Kat?"

Kat never looked up from what she was doing and replied, "Oh, yeah, I knew. I knew from the beginning."

"Ok," Noah nodded. "Good. Then tell me what you know."

"Why?" Kat smirked. "Why would you want to know any of it?"

"Because I do. The thought of Melissa being sick and having no one really bothers me."

Kat slammed the shaker in her hand on the table and looked up at Noah. "Does it now? Does it really bother you? You? Noah Litchfield?"

"Of course it does! Damn, Kat. What kind of person do you think I am?"

"I don't know, Noah. Why don't you tell me? Because what I know of you is you're just a player. You played almost every woman in this town, including *me*, and you played Melissa in a *big* way."

Noah sighed. "I know I did. And I deserve that. I was a jerk. But you knew that beforehand.

But if I'd known that she was sick, I could've done something."

"Like what? Leave Dr. Blaylock so you could take care of Melissa? Like that was ever gonna happen...." Kat sneered.

"No. I wouldn't have stopped seeing Maddie. But together, she and I could've done so much for Melissa. You know that."

"No. What I know is that you don't own up to your responsibilities and Melissa was one responsibility you wouldn't have wanted. That I do know for sure."

"What responsibilities? Melissa wasn't my responsibility, but I wouldn't have walked away either had I known she was sick."

"Yeah, well, that's all water under the bridge now, isn't it?"

They were silent for a few minutes as Noah milled over what Kat had told him. "So tell me...when did she find out she had cancer?" Noah asked eventually.

"I'm not sure exactly, but I think it was about a week or so before ya'll starting seeing each other."

"God, why didn't she say something then?"

"She was going to. But ya'll didn't see each other long enough for her to tell you. What was it? A week or two? She never could find a way to tell you and when she was ready to talk about it, you started seeing Dr. Blaylock. So what was the point then?"

"Can you tell me where the cancer was?" Noah asked softly.

"Breast cancer. Both breasts. By the time she found the lump, it was practically too late. All the tests showed it was in her lymph nodes, too."

"Geez...how awful. When did she leave the Cope?"

"About a month or so later. Went to New Jersey to see some doctor. Some herbalist or homeopathic doctor, I'm not sure."

"Why on earth would she go to a doctor like that? Didn't she get treatment here, radiation, chemo, all that stuff?"

"Well, they started out doing a double mastectomy, but when it was time to start the chemo and radiation, she backed out. She didn't want it."

"What?? Why would she not have the treatments?"

"Would it have saved her life, Noah? You think so? She was too far gone," Kat said shaking her head.

"It might have prolonged her life. Given her more time. How could she not give herself that chance?"

Kat shook her head. "Look, I don't know what Melissa was thinking, or that she was thinking at all. All I can say is, I've told you too much now and I promised her I'd never tell you anything."

"Why? Why didn't she want me to know? Why was it some big secret?"

"Noah, look...it's none of your business now and it was never any of your business. She didn't want you to know. End of story. So you can go on now and marry the doctor and have lots of other babies and have a great life. Okay?" Kat stood up from the booth and moved to walk away from Noah. Noah sat there for a second, Kat's words ringing in his head. *Other babies? Other babies?*

Noah stood up quickly and grabbed Kat by the arm and swung her around to face him.

"*Other* babies, Kat? What the hell are you talking about?" Noah's heart was racing.

"Nothing, Noah. Nothing. Dammit now, I've got work to do and I'm done talking to you."

"Huh uh....woman, you aren't done talking to me," Noah held onto Kat by both her shoulders and lifted her up to his eye level. "You tell me, *right now*, what you mean by *other* babies. Are you telling me she was pregnant?"

Kat fought her way out of Noah's grip and backed away from him. "I'm not telling you anything." She pointed towards the door, "Now get the hell outa here and forget you ever talk to me!" Sadie had come from the kitchen and was shaking her head.

"Now look hare, ya two! Ya'll jis betta calm down and lowah ya mouts...."

Noah looked at Kat and his voice softened. "Kat, please...."

Kat's eyes welled up with tears and she fervently shook her head. "Forget it, Noah. I gave my word."

Sadie spoke up again. "Now, gal, if'n ya knows sumptin' dat boy dare need da know, ya bes git to tellin' him. Dat dare kinda news ain't sumptin' ya keep from a man."

"Kat, what are you trying to tell me...was she pregnant or not?" Noah pleaded with her.

Kat threw her hands up in the air. "FINE, okay, she was pregnant! Happy now? She was pregnant with *your* kid and she didn't want you to know!"

Noah's legs went out from under him and he

fell back into the booth. “What? Why? How could she not tell me....” He put his head in his hands.

Kat sat back in the booth with Noah and took a deep breath. “She didn’t want you to know because she knew you’d marry her, when you didn’t really love her just to have the kid. Or she thought you’d try and take the baby if you didn’t marry her and that kid was all she had left in the world.”

“So what did she do? Did she have an abortion? She decided instead to kill our unborn child??” Noah was frantic.

“Lawd, have mercy on dis hare man,” Sadie raised her hands and face to the heavens. “Gib dis man strenth, gawd, da git shrew dis.” She walked into the back of the kitchen and left them alone.

Kat shook her head. “No, Noah, she didn’t have an abortion. That’s why she didn’t take the radiation and stuff...she wanted to keep the baby safe. She had the baby."

Noah slowly looked up from his hands. *Did she just say Melissa had the baby? I have a child somewhere?* "She had the baby?"

Kat nodded slowly. "She went to Jersey to see that quack doctor and stayed in a shelter for unwed mothers...it was hard on her. Her body just wilted away to nothing, but she still hung on until the baby was born. She lived only three days after she had the baby."

Noah swallowed hard as the room began to spin around him. "I have a child somewhere in this world, and you two thought I didn't need to *know?*"

Kat wiped the tears from her face. "Noah, it was so hard not telling you, but I was made to promise, on Melissa's death bed, not to ever tell you. She was so head-strong, even in the last days, and she was the only true friend I had...how could I betray her?"

"So you betray me instead?"

"I didn't know what to do."

"Maybe it isn't mine. Maybe that's why she didn't tell me. That's a strong possibility."

"No, it was yours. She hadn't been with anyone for months before you and by the time you started seeing Dr. Blaylock, she was already pregnant. She just didn't know it."

Noah was trying to gather his thoughts, make a plan, *how in the world will I tell Maddie, my parents...*"So what did she do with the baby? Where is it? What is it?"

"As far as I know, the women at the shelter were going to keep it for now. She left pretty solid instructions that it wasn't to be put up for adoption, if possible. She said she'd gotten really close to the people that ran the shelter and she could leave this world knowing her child was being raised in a loving place. A place she knew, with people she knew. Melissa said she couldn't spend an eternity in hell not knowing where her child was. *Hell*, she thought she was going to hell, can you imagine that?"

Noah stood up from the booth. "I want the name of the shelter, Kat. I want to know where my child is. If it is my child, it's not growing up in a shelter."

"*He*, Noah, *he's* not growing up in a shelter. You have a son," Kat whispered.

"I have a son..." Noah said softly. "A boy..."

Kat took her pen and wrote something on a napkin and handed it to Noah. "I will probably burn in hell for telling you all of this, but I think I'm doing the right thing." She turned to walk away and stopped. "If you go through with this, will you please tell those people at the shelter that I only did what I thought was best for the boy?"

"Yeah, that I can tell them. What I won't be able to tell them is why you waited so long. If I hadn't found out about Melissa, you would have never told me, would you have?"

Kat shrugged her shoulders. "I don't know. But that's a pointless question now, isn't it?"

****

Noah left the café and immediately dialed Julian's cell phone. If anybody could stop a legal proceeding of any kind, it was Julian. He was in the Wrangler, headed home when Julian picked up.

"Julian? Noah."

"Little brother, what's up now?"

"I need a big favor and I need you to keep your mouth shut about it for awhile. Can you do that?"

"How many times have I before?"

Noah overlooked the sarcasm in Julian's voice and looked at the napkin Kat had given him. "I need you to make a phone call. 756-555-4521. *The Sun Will Come Up Shelter*. Jersey. You find out who's in charge of the place and tell them that *if* there are any legal proceedings regarding a male infant born to the late Melissa Wells, those proceedings are to stop immediately."

"Noah, I can't stop any proceedings without a court order."

"Well then, I suggest you tell them you have one and then get your ass in gear and get one."

"Do I even want to ask how this involves you?" Julian asked.

"Probably not. But I'll tell you everything later today. I've got to get on a plane to Jersey."

"Jesus Christ."

"Thanks, Julian."

"You're welcome. *Again.*"

****

Maddie was on the phone with Moby when Noah pulled up in the drive. She watched him step out of the jeep and caught her breath. He still made her heart skip a beat and she couldn't believe they were going to be married in just a few months. Then she saw the look on his face and she knew his visit with Kat had not gone well. "Moby, hon, I'm gonna have to call you back. Noah's just coming home and I know he's going to want to tell me all about his visit with Kat. Tell all hello....love you." Maddie clicked off the cordless just as Noah was opening the door. He leaned down and gave her a soft kiss and a big hug.

Sweet Dreams, Doc

"Hey baby...how'd it go?" Maddie asked. Noah sighed heavily and sat down at the kitchen counter and pulled out a stool for Maddie to join him.

"I don't even know where to begin," he said slowly.

"The beginning. The beginning would be a good place."

He let out a long sigh and looked at Maddie. "Well, for starters, it was breast cancer. By the time they found it, it was in her lymph nodes." Maddie shuddered. "They did a double mastectomy, but she refused any radiation or chemo. She ended up in New Jersey because of some holistic doctor there. She lived at a shelter the whole time."

"Why did she refuse treatment? I mean, I know it wouldn't have cured the cancer, but it might have given her a little more time."

Noah reached over and took Maddie's hand in his. "Doc, oh god, this is so hard." She ran her hand up his back and squeezed her other hand tightly in his. "Baby, it's okay. It's going to be okay," she whispered.

"Maddie, she refused the treatment because she was pregnant," Noah couldn't look Maddie in the eye as he said it.

Maddie looked at him and whispered again, "She was pregnant? Oh, Noah, she did it for the baby? How honorable and careless at the same time."

"Baby, you're not hearing me. She was *pregnant.*"

Her eyes grew larger and she shook her head gently, "Noah, tell me this child wasn't yours..."

He couldn't answer her, he only sat there in

silence. Maddie let his hand go and stood from the stool. She walked around the counter into the kitchen and leaned onto the sink for support. She gazed out of the window and looked out over the Atlantic. Without turning to face him, she spoke so softly Noah barely heard her, "Where is this child now?"

Noah cleared his throat before he answered. "As far as I know, he's at the shelter in Jersey."

Never turning around, Maddie replied, "Then you have to go get him. You can't leave him there. If he truly is your son, you have to go get him." Noah went to her then and turned her to face him. "How could I have messed up so badly?" he whispered as he took her in his arms. He was crying now and so ashamed, embarrassed, heartbroken, all mixed together. He knew he had broken Maddie's heart as well and that in itself broke his heart.

Maddie looked up at him and wiped a tear from his eye as she blinked her own away. "You messed up royally. You used Melissa because of me and for that, I share some of the guilt. She chose not to tell you, and that's not your fault. You can't feel guilty for something you had no knowledge of. But if you walk away from this child without at least finding out if he is your son, then you will really have messed up."

"Maddie, what will we do if this boy is mine? How do we, you and I, go on from here? Where will a child fit into our lives?"

"Noah Litchfield, let me tell you something right now. If that boy is yours, he will be *ours* and we will go on as planned. We'll still get married, we'll have more children later. Children were always in the plan, maybe not so soon, but in the plan regardless. We'll make it work; but letting go of your past and putting this child behind us is not in the plan. I'll never be the same if we don't go get him."

CHAPTER EIGHTEEN

The next morning they were on a plane to New Jersey. Julian made the call to *The Sun Will Come Up Shelter* and found out there was indeed an infant residing there born to Melissa. There were no legal proceedings taking place and the court order tucked into Noah's coat pocket was all he needed to stop any.

The counselor at the shelter knew Noah and Maddie were on their way and had agreed to meet with them that afternoon. Maddie closed the office for the next few days, only saying it was a family emergency, and had instructed Caroline and Alline to send any patients to the next town if they needed a doctor or to the ER of the hospital if they needed tending.

Noah told his parents and Julia what was going on and was certain his father and mother would be devastated. His mother had simply hugged him and told him to bring the child home if indeed he was a Litchfield and his father had agreed. "No need in worrying now about gossip or speculation, son. Go to the boy and see for yourself. You're not the first and you won't be the last to have a moment's lapse of judgment. Go to the child," Kirkland had instructed.

The taxi pulled up in front of the shelter a little after four in the afternoon. Noah was so nervous he thought he would vomit all over the sidewalk and Maddie wasn't doing much better. "I think I'll know, doc, the minute I see him. I'll know if he's mine or not," he whispered as they walked through the front door. "I know you will," Maddie whispered back.

Neither were expecting the shelter to be what it really was. A home. They walked right into a living room to find several young women, all pregnant, relaxed and comfortable, reading, watching TV, doing crossword puzzles, like so many other young women in their own homes.

"Hello. Can any of you tell me where I might find, " Noah looked down at the piece of paper in his hand, "Mrs. Tate?"

"Sure," one of the young girls replied. "I'll get her for you." She rose slowly, with her back bowed from the weight of her growing belly and walked out of the room. The rest of the women stared at them and finally another spoke. "You're Noah, aren't you?"

Startled, Noah replied, "Yes, yes I am. How did you know that?"

The same girl answered, smiling. "She talked about you all the time. Melissa. She described you to a tee. She wasn't lying either."

Noah smiled a little. "Well, I don't know if

that's a good thing or a bad thing, depending on what she told you." Maddie could only imagine what Melissa had said about her.

"Nah, it wouldn't all bad. She said she wasn't no good for you. That it was what it was, but that you'd always been good to her. Talked about you, too, that is if you're the lady doctor," she continued, looking at Maddie.

Maddie smiled also. "Yes, I'm the lady doctor, Maddie."

"Yeah, she said you was pretty, too. Said you were the kinda lady Noah should be with."

"That was kind of her. I'm sure being here wasn't easy for her, being sick and alone," Maddie said softly.

"Well, she weren't ever alone, m'am. That's one thing she wasn't."

The first young woman had fetched Mrs.

Tate, who walked briskly through the door with her. She was in her late fifties and plump. She had a cheerful smile on her face and reached to shake hands with Noah and Maddie.

"Hello! I'm Mrs. Tate, and you must be Noah and Maddie. Won't you come with me into my office? We'll have more privacy there." She gestured for the two to follow her. They settled in comfortable chairs in front of her desk and Mrs. Tate opened a folder.

"I supposed you'd be here sooner or later. I didn't really know how long Melissa's friend could keep such a secret," Mrs. Tate began.

"Mrs. Tate," Noah began, "I want you to know that had I known from day one, the situation, I would have been here. I had no idea that Melissa had left South Carolina, much less that she was sick *or* pregnant." Mrs. Tate was nodding her head.

"I know, son. Melissa told me everything and I don't hold any ill will against you. To be honest, I was already working up the nerve to call you myself. Dying wish, or no dying wish, if this child is yours, he deserves to be with his father and you, dear, deserve to be with him."

Maddie spoke up, "I don't want to sound cruel or judgmental, but Noah and I have discussed the fact that we'd like a paternity test. Just to be sure. We wouldn't want to take the child as our own if his father is someone else." Mrs. Tate raised an eyebrow and Maddie quickly continued. "We wouldn't want another man to be unaware that he has a child. We wouldn't want to take that life from him as well."

"I agree with you, Dr. Blaylock. I think we should do just that. If you'll pardon me for just a moment, I'll make a phone call and see how fast we can get the test done." She picked up the phone and make arrangements for the test in the next hour.

"Now, with that done, would you like to see the child? I mean, we can wait until the paternity is determined, if you like."

Noah and Maddie thought about that for a minute and they both smiled. "We'd like to see him now, if we could," Noah said.

"Absolutely you can. Follow me," Mrs. Tate said, rising from her chair. They walked down the hall to a small bedroom. It had been made into a nursery and the crib was just in front of the double windows where the sun could shine brightly on its precious contents. Noah stopped just inside the door and looked up at the ceiling.

"Maddie....what if...." his voice trailed off.

"No," Maddie replied, taking his hand. "No what ifs. Take a deep breath."

****

Together they walked toward the crib and looked at the baby, sleeping peacefully. Noah watched his tiny chest rise and fall with each breath, his little chin quiver ever so often as he dreamed and his small, pink lips purse as if looking for a bottle.

One tiny hand was on top of the blanket that cradled him and his fingers were long like Noah's. The infant had just a wisp of chestnut hair and neither Maddie nor Noah overlooked the fact that he had a dimple in his chin...just like Noah.

Mrs. Tate left them alone with the baby allowing them the time they needed to get adjusted to this idea.

"Noah, he's beautiful..." Maddie whispered.

"Yes, he is. And I know he's mine, doc. I know. I can feel it in my chest. I feel like I'm having a heart attack." Maddie smiled up at him.

"I want to hold him..." Maddie whispered again. She reached into the crib and gently lifted the baby into her arms. The child immediately grunted like a puppy as he snuggled under her neck.

"Did you hear that?" she giggled.

"Yeah, is he okay? Do they do that?" Noah asked nervously.

"Yeah, baby, they do that, " she giggled again.

Maddie slowly sat down in the rocking chair beside the crib and gently rocked the chair back and forth. Noah knelt down by her and softly caressed the baby's small head. He leaned in and kissed him quietly on his forehead and immediately started crying. "God, Maddie, how could a screw-up like me create such a beautiful child?"

"Noah, hush right now. You are not a

screw-up. This child is proof of that. *I'm proof of that.* Our life together is proof of that." She stood up and handed the boy to Noah, carefully showing him how to cradle the baby's head. Noah's tears were flowing freely down his face and falling gently onto the baby.

"What are we going to do if he's not mine?" Noah stopped short.

"We're going to take him home anyway. We'll do what we can to find his real father and then try our best to adopt him anyway. I can't leave him here and I know you can't either."

Mrs. Tate walked in, followed by a nurse. "Okie dokie, Mr. Litchfield, this is Ms. Patterson and she'll be administering the paternity test," she informed.

The nurse took a swab from the packet and asked Noah to open his mouth. She very quickly swabbed the inside of one cheek and then the other.

After placing the swab in a sterile container, she opened a new swab and swabbed the inside of the baby's mouth as well. "That's it. We're all done. Give me a day or two and you'll have your answer." Ms. Patterson quickly exited the room, leaving them with Mrs. Tate and the baby. Maddie stood next to Noah, taking note of all the similarities the baby shared with Noah. There was no doubt in her mind that this child was indeed a Litchfield.

Noah softly caressed the baby's small head and looked to Mrs. Tate. "Does he have a name? Did Melissa name him?"

Mrs. Tate simply shook her head. "She only called him Little One, and it's pretty much stuck with all of us. His birth certificate does list her and yourself, as the parents, but as of yet, he remains unnamed. Maybe she thought we would eventually name him," Mrs. Tate sighed. "Personally, I feel she thought you'd come for him in the end and name him yourself."

CHAPTER NINETEEN

They asked for and were given, the name of the cemetery where Melissa was laid to rest just weeks before. After leaving the baby in the care of Mrs. Tate, they took a cab to the small public graveyard just twenty minutes from the shelter. The cemetery was one for indigents, where burials were paid for by the state, but it was clean and kept neat, if simple. With some help from the caretaker, Maddie and Noah found Melissa's grave site with little trouble. Her final resting place was marked by a simple black marker with letters and numbers that slid in and out of the plate.

Noah dropped his head when they found the spot and sighed heavily. "I can't believe she's lying here among these people. She deserves better......"

"Noah, it's not that bad really. At least it's kept up and cleaned." Maddie whispered.

He shook his head. "But she's out here with homeless people and drunks and god knows what else."

Maddie took his hand in hers and held it tightly. "You want to bring her back to the Cope?"

Noah looked at Maddie for a long time before answering. "I think so. Even if this child isn't mine, I think she deserves to be back in South Carolina. Among people who knew her, where she had friends..."

They left the cemetery and while en route to their hotel had decided to let Mrs. Tate know that regardless of the paternity, they wanted to take the little one home with them and they would pursue his paternity and seek adoption. Noah called the shelter from his cell phone and after speaking to Mrs. Tate, he called Julian. Julian had promised to have orders drawn up to have Melissa's body exhumed in order to bring her back to South

Carolina.

By now he'd been informed by the elder Litchfields of Noah's dilemma but was surprisingly supportive of his little brother's wishes. It would take several days to have it done, but that was okay. Noah and Maddie knew they weren't leaving New Jersey without the little one and without Melissa.

After stopping at the shelter and spending a few hours with the baby, they headed back to their suite at the hotel. Noah's head was spinning and he felt like he was in a movie trailer. "I can't believe just two days ago I had no knowledge of any of this." He snuggled up to Maddie on the sofa in the living room part of their suite.

Maddie sighed. "Neither can I. I can't believe two days ago, I was only worried about planning a wedding. Now all of that seems so trivial."

"Baby, I'm so sorry to have ruined this for you. I know you have all of these big plans and it should be such a special time and now it's tainted by a new baby and taking a dead woman back home."

"Noah, stop. Our wedding day hasn't been tainted. It will still be the most important day of my life...the happiest day of my life. This has just shown me how little it will be compared to this. I mean, this is *big.*"

"I hope so, doc. I just can't believe after all these years of running, I've finally found what I was looking for and now, this wrench gets thrown in. I don't know what I was thinking asking you to accept all of this and be a part of this mess. You deserve so much more than my screw-ups...."

Maddie wrapped her arms tightly around Noah and whispered to him, "Noah, don't you see?

God had a plan for us, He had a plan for that baby and it was always in the works. This is where we are meant to be right now...doing this. And I love you more now than I ever have. The Noah I knew a year ago would have run like a bat out of hell from this type of situation and look at you now...." She leaned up and kissed his softly. "You're fighting like hell for a child that may or may not be yours and pulling all kind of strings to get his dead mother back to the Cope."

They spent the rest of the next day at the shelter getting to know the little one. Noah wanted to name him so badly, but in his heart he had to know first. It was selfish of him, he knew, but before he could give this boy the Litchfield name he yearned to give him, he wanted to know.

Mrs. Tate had opened her arms and her heart to them and was so happy to see them take to the child with no reservations. She was even more happy to know that they had decided to exhume the Wells girl and take her back to South Carolina. It was God's work at hand and surely meant to be.

On the third day of their trip to Jersey, they were met by Mrs. Tate at the shelter as soon as they walked through the door that morning.

"It's here! It's here! The paternity test is here..." She was pacing back and forth. She hurriedly rushed them into her office and closed the door. Noah couldn't sit, even after Mrs. Tate asked him to several times and Maddie was glad to sit. She was sure she would vomit on the floor, she was so nervous. Mrs. Tate fiddled with the envelope and wasn't sure she'd ever get it open. When she did, she scanned all the customary mumbo jumbo, quickly finding the sentence she was looking for. She read it to herself first and then smiled as big as the horizon.

Nervously, she read out loud, "In the case of

the male infant born to Melissa Wells, paternity has been determined that Noah Litchfield is 99.99% the biological father of said infant." She threw her hands up in the air and let out a little whoop.

Noah dropped to his knees and gathered Maddie in his arms, crying openly. Maddie wrapped her arms about him and whispered, "Shhh, it's okay, baby, he's ours. He's ours now."

They walked into the nursery arm in arm and Noah picked up the little one from his crib. He held his son close to him and smelled his baby smell deeply. He cried openly to the point of shaking and Maddie couldn't help but cry too.

"Hello, little one," Noah whispered in the baby's ear. "I'm your daddy and this is your mommy. We're so glad we found you."

After a tearful goodbye to Mrs. Tate and the girls at the shelter, they left for their hotel with what little belongings the baby had. An hour later, they were stretched out on the bed with the baby sleeping peacefully between them. The little one cooed in his sleep and a tiny smile curled on his pink lips. His tiny chin quivered in contentment.

Maddie reached over and took Noah's hand. "You know, I think it's time *little one* gets a name, don't you?"

"Yeah, I was just thinking the same thing. I always wanted my first born son to have my name, but I'm not so sure now." Noah signed.

"Why not, baby?"

"Because. I know this isn't going to sound too great, but I kind of wanted *our* child to have my name."

"Noah. He is *our* child. What's wrong with you? I'm the only mommy he's ever going to have and he will always be our first born child."

"Really? You don't mind if we name him after me?" Noah smiled.

"Of course not. In fact, I was already thinking the same thing. With one exception."

"And what is that exception?" Noah asked, smiling.

"I think we should include Melissa's name. That way she'll always be a part of him."

"You want us to name our son *Melissa?*" Noah grinned.

"No, you dope. I think we should name him, *Noah Reed Wells Litchfield.*"

Noah's grin broadened. "I love it. What will we call him? Reed?"

Maddie shrugged her shoulders. "I don't know. I kind of like Wells. That way we won't ever forget and I think it will help him understand just how much his birth mother was cared for and remembered."

"I would have never thought of that and here you are, taking into your heart another woman's child and insisting he have her name. Have I told you how much I love you?"

****

They'd been in New Jersey for five days when the orders to exhume Melissa arrived via fax to the public affairs office. Within a matter of hours, Noah had a contractor at the cemetery. He couldn't bear to watch the actual exhumation, but was waiting at the airport when the team arrived.

Melissa's coffin had been placed inside a new vault and was ready for the flight back to South Carolina by late that afternoon. The following morning, Noah, Maddie and Wells boarded a plane back home with Wells' birth mother safely resting in the belly of the plane.

The new family arrived safely, and at their request, with no fanfare, at the Charleston airport around lunchtime. Noah had made arrangements for the funeral director from Canton Cope to meet them in Charleston and take Melissa back to the coast. He and Maddie would make final arrangements once they settled in back home.

Before beginning their drive back to the Cope, they stopped by the cemetery so that Maddie's parents could meet Wells. It was a tearful visit, but once again Maddie was sure she could hear her mother's soft whisper, "*you did good, Maddie. Now spread your wings and embrace this child...*"

The fanfare that wasn't allowed at the airport awaited them at Maddie's house in full grandeur. Kirkland, Jestine, Julia, Hamp, Moby and

Clint were at the house with cameras and flowers, balloons and more baby stuff than Maddie had ever seen in her life. Even Jasper and Sadie had arrived with homemade apple sauce and a jar of Sadie's own recipe of a colic cure-all . There were tears aplenty, but happy tears and smiles and laughter and all the love little Wells could have ever imagined. It was a homecoming they would share with him countless times in his lifetime.

Julia and Moby had pulled out all the stops for his nursery, painting the room a baby blue and filling it with all the essentials a new baby would need. From a crib, changing table, rocking chair, chest of drawers full of clothes, not to mention the closet full, diapers, formula, toys, stuffed animals, it was all there. Moby had even painted a mural on one wall depicting a scene from the children's story of Peter Pan. She thought it more than appropriate that this little lost boy know the story of the real lost boys. Maddie and Noah couldn't have agreed more.

The next few days were a blur as more family and friends poured into the house and brought more gifts. Little Wells was surely a gift from God as he was already sleeping through the night and knew well the difference in his days and his nights. Maddie was certain she was missing out on something by not having to get up two and three times a night, but all the mothers assured her she was quite fortunate. It didn't keep her or Noah from waking in the night nonetheless and sneaking into his nursery off and on just to make sure he was breathing.

****

The weekend following their arrival home, they held a small, quiet service at the church cemetery for Melissa and were happy to see a rather large crowd attended. When the service was over and Melissa was at last resting again, Kat Simmons made her way through the crowd to reach Noah and

Maddie. Noah reached out and hugged Kat and thanked her for coming.

"I also want to thank you from the bottom of my heart for telling me about Wells. I can't imagine my life without him now and I owe it all to you," Noah said, smiling at Kat.

"Kat, you did a good thing," Maddie agreed. "I know Melissa is happy that Noah has their son and I know she's glad you told Noah everything."

Kat smiled. "I guess you're right. I hated that I couldn't keep her dyin' wish, but I think she's lookin' down now and she's happy with the way it all turned out. I know she's real glad to be back here, you know, where she can see everybody and keep an eye on Wells. Which by the way, I think it's real cool you named him after her. She'd be real proud." Her eyes welled up. "I miss her a lot."

"I'm sure you do," Maddie gave her a little hug. "And please know, that anytime you want to come see Wells, you are more than welcome. You knew Melissa after all and we want him to know her, too."

"Really?" Kat asked, a little surprised.

"Of course," Noah replied. "He'll know all about Melissa and where he came from and how brave she was in keeping him safe. He'll know it all, as only we think he should. How many women would be that brave in the face of their own life or death?"

"Wow. You really are a pretty decent guy, Noah." Kat said.

Maddie and Noah laughed softly. "Well, thank you for that, Kat," Noah placed a hand on her back.

Sweet Dreams, Doc

CHAPTER TWENTY

The next Sunday Noah and Maddie decided to have Wells christened that morning during services. They thought at first they should wait until after they were married, but the pastor had assured them that under the circumstances, God would understand and in fact, would probably be more than pleased to welcome Wells into the church now. Again the church was full of family and friends, even Julian and Celeste and the kids had come from D.C. to be a part of the event.

Noah and Maddie, with Wells in their arms, joined the pastor at the front of the church. Wells was adorned in his father's christening gown and wore Maddie's father's crucifix around his neck.

"Friends, family, loved ones, God's family - we are proud today, to present to you and in the presence of our Holy Father, this little one. This child of God. His parents, Noah Litchfield, and Dr. Madison Blaylock, " the pastor paused, looked at Maddie and smiled, "the soon to be Mrs. Dr. Madison Litchfield, have come today to present to God and these loved ones, little Noah Reed Wells Litchfield." Maddie carefully cradled Wells in the pastor's arms and took Noah's hand, as the pastor continued.

As he sprinkled holy water on the child's chest, he spoke. "We give this child, Wells Litchfield, unto you, God. Place him in your loving arms and guide his spirit through this world." The pastor dipped his thumb into the vat of holy water and made the mark of the cross on Wells' forehead. "I baptize thee, Noah Reed Wells Litchfield, in the name of the Father, the Son and the Holy Ghost. As we are witnesses to this child's dedication to our Lord in Heaven, so we also are committing to guide him throughout this life to follow our Creator's path, commandments and scriptures all the days of his life. Amen."

In the course of one week, Noah and Maddie had flown out of state, brought home a child and his deceased mother, planned and carried out her funeral, finalized Maddie's adoption of the child and then baptized that child before God and their loved ones. It was more than they could take and by the beginning of the next week, they were exhausted. Noah was thankful it was the off-season and Maddie was grateful for the nurse practitioner that had agreed to fill in for her at the office for the next few weeks. *Who knew you could have maternity leave without giving birth*? Maddie thought as she roused up Monday morning to the smell of fresh coffee.

Noah was seated at the kitchen counter, the morning paper spread out in front of him, Wells rocking quietly in the battery-operated swing in front the picture window. He had a great view of the harbor and was soaking up the warm sun that shone through the panes. "You're already showing him the shrimp boats?" Maddie laughed, kissing Noah on the top of the head. She walked over to Wells and leaned in to kiss the top of his as well.

"Well, of course. No time like the present. He might as well know where he'll be spending the rest of his life, if he chooses to." Noah smiled.

"I don't know about you, but I feel like I've been run over by a train. Is it just me, or have we had one helluva week?" Maddie sighed with a smile.

"Yeah, babe. It's been one helluva week. Come here." He motioned for her to sit on his leg and she gladly accepted. "I love you so much it hurts sometimes. And I am the luckiest man on the earth. I don't want you to ever forget that." Noah drew her close and kissed her softly, letting it linger for a minute or two.

"I think *we're* the luckiest people on the earth and I love you more and more each day. I feel so blessed right now, even amidst all the sore muscles, tired bones, hectic weeks, all that crap, I am so blessed." Maddie rested her head on his shoulder. "You know when my parents died, I was so alone. Other than Moby, I was basically orphaned. Other than a few cousins that I rarely see, Moby was my family. Now in the blink of an eye, I have this huge family, extended family and more friends than I can count. And now, this little guy. Talk about blessed."

Sweet Dreams, Doc

CHAPTER TWENTY-ONE

The weeks turned into months and before they both knew it, their wedding day was just days away. The ceremony would be held at their church in the town square and the reception would be at The Veranda. There had been no limits to the festivities and it promised to be *the* event of the year. Simon Salley had happily agreed to let Sadie assist in the catering and she was as busy as a bee preparing many delectable treats for the wedding party and guests.

Maddie had selected her bridesmaids - Moby would be Maid of Honor, Julia, Celeste, Alline, Kat and Tisha, Jasper's wife, and Mary Grace would be a junior bridesmaid. Noah has chosen his best man, obviously, to be his father Kirkland and his groomsmen to be Julian, Clint, Hamp, Jasper and Sumpter and Kirk as junior groomsman.

Sweet Dreams, Doc

Wells was now a plump, rambunctious 10 month old. He was walking already and into everything. He was babbling away all the time now and his parents relished in hearing him call, "ma ma, da da" with every breath. Maddie took him to work with her until he reached five months old at which time, they enlisted the help of Sadie and Kat, who took turns keeping him at the cottage.

Kat was never happier than when she sat for Wells and in her quirky way, felt that Melissa was watching over them. Sadie was intent on getting Wells to say her name and it came out 'A E', which she loved immediately. From that moment on, she was known simply as AE and was certain her future grandchildren would pick it up, too. They weren't sure how well he would do, but Maddie and Noah knew he had to be their ring bearer. They could only hope for the best.

****

Noah opened his eyes around five a.m. the morning of his wedding and lay still, listening to Maddie breathing peacefully, still deeply asleep. Wells had spent the night at his grandparents' house with his young cousins so that Maddie and Noah would have the day to prepare.

Although unconventional, they had decided to spend the night together and spend the day together rather than go with the old tradition of not seeing each other the day of their marriage. Noah didn't think he could've stood going all day without Maddie around anyway and he was certain she felt the same.

He rose up on one elbow and watched her heart beat as she silently slept. Gently he brushed the hair from her face and traced the outline of her jaw line with the back of his hand. Without hesitation, he leaned over to her and softly kissed the fullness of her lips and waited on her to rouse.

Sweet Dreams, Doc

Maddie smiled without opening her eyes and whispered, “good morning, handsome man.”

Noah smiled back. “Good morning, Mrs. Litchfield.”

“Not yet, goober.”

“Close enough, doc. Wake up and love me...” he whispered, seductively.

“Are you trying to ruin me for my husband? I can’t go to my marriage bed a tainted woman.” She still hadn’t opened her eyes, but she was still smiling.

He reached under the covers and gently laid his hand on the softness between her legs, gingerly caressing the silk of her panties and the growing moistness beneath. He brushed his lips against her ear, “I won’t tell if you won’t tell...”

“In that case,” Maddie hoarsely replied, “take my panties off and have your way with me.”

In one swift pull, Noah slid her wet panties from her hips as she slipped her t-shirt over her head. She reached down for his boxer briefs and tugged until he was free of them. Still facing each other, they embraced, kissing softly, taking their time. Today, there would be no rushing, no hurrying and no frantic deadlines. The plans were made, the people prepared, the clothes pressed and the flowers ordered. Today was their day to relish in their moment.

Noah lowered his head to let his mouth find her breasts, full and erect, eager for his touch. He slipped his hand between her legs and continued his erotic massage until he could feel the swelled lips of her womanhood. Maddie covered his neck in kisses and nibbles while her own hand found his hardness dripping with excitement. They continued their play, taking time to delve into each other's bodies, relaxed in each other's arms and patient to make it last as long as it could.

After nearly an hour of fondling, and cuddling, and tasting, Maddie climbed on top of Noah and gently lowered herself onto his throbbing cock. Slowly, she let him enter her, easing herself down just a little and then lifting herself almost completely off him and back down again. With each in and out move, she squeezed her muscles tighter to heighten his pleasure and he moaned in appreciative response.

Noah reached around her and let his hand rest against the small area of her stomach, as his thumb found her clit and with each move of her hips, he stroked it. Back and forth, round and round, she rode him softly, gently, taking her time and lingering in the ecstasy that was love making with Noah. He sat up and let his mouth find hers as she continued to ride him, his hands palming her breasts, his mouth then finding her nipples.

Maddie's breaths were getting shorter and her hips were moving faster and she was close to letting go. Noah eased back on the bed and found her clit again, which sent her into a frenzy as she pumped her mound into him harder and harder.

She arched her back just as she released herself into him and he reached to embrace her. Noah then gently laid her on the bed and spread her legs with his knees. She was still trembling with glorious waves of ecstasy as he entered her again. Maddie spread her legs wide, wanting him deeper inside her and lifted her hips off the bed to meet his thrusts.

He could feel her tighten around his cock with each stroke and it drove him mad with desire. She lifted her head to kiss him and they locked lips in a fierce kiss, tongues diving and tasting. Maddie was ready again to explode as she called out his name, Noah, ready himself to spill his seed deep into her. With one last shudder and a growl from deep in his throat, he gave in to the physical impact and together they came in waves of pleasure.

Breathless and entwined in an embrace neither was eager to be rid of, they smiled and giggled at what their pastor may say of their morning tryst. "I don't think we're being very nice right now," Maddie giggled. "We shouldn't be so ugly. But then again, we are about to be married, right?"

"Absolutely. And as far as I'm concerned, I'm marrying a virgin."

"Yeah, uh-huh....sure you are. And I'm marrying a saint," Maddie smiled.

They lingered an hour or so more and eventually peeled away from each other to take a joint shower, where they again consummated a marriage that had yet to happen. Reluctantly, they parted ways at lunch time. Maddie headed to the elder Litchfields for her bridal luncheon with her bridesmaids and a scattering of friends and Noah headed to the Yacht Club to dine with his groomsman and a few friends.

Within hours, they were headed to the church in the square for the biggest night of their lives. They kissed goodbye at the limos and promised to see each other shortly.

Sweet Dreams, Doc

CHAPTER TWENTY-TWO

At ten minutes before the hour of six, the doors to the vestibule opened and the groomsman and bridesmaids took their places. Wells made his way haphazardly down the aisle with his pillow in hand, until his spotted his Daddy at the altar. At which time, he took off running and jumped into Noah's arms and the congregation burst into laughter.

The doors were then closed and at six o'clock sharp, the bells in the church tower tolled six times. Noah held his breath and could hear his heart beating outside his chest as waited for the doors to open again. When they did, he lost his breath completely and he was sure his heart stopped for a split second. There Maddie stood in the most beautiful dress he'd ever seen.

She was breathtaking in a gown of pure silk,

ivory in color, full skirt, thin shoulder straps that just teased the sides of her arms. The dress was covered in seed pearls and the bodice was gathered in lace that gave an amazing show of her plentiful cleavage. Maddie had chosen a short veil of organza that gathered at the crown of her head with a tiara of pearls. In her hands, she carried a bouquet of white cannas tied with a simple ribbon of ivory silk. Beneath that bouquet and unseen by the congregation, Noah knew she was also carrying her mother's tiny Bible and her father's handkerchief.

Moby was with her, at her side, as Maddie had asked her to give her away. Together they walked down the aisle, Moby was crying softly and Maddie was trying her best not to. When they reached the alter and the pastor asked who gave this woman to be wed, Moby barely whispered, "On behalf of her parents, Austin and Lillian Blaylock, I very proudly and happily give this woman to be wed." With that said, she kissed Maddie's cheek, stepped aside and took Maddie's flowers to her side.

Noah took Maddie's hands in his own and together they looked at their pastor and waited anxiously to exchange their vows. Silently and unbeknownst to the guests, Noah and Maddie whispered sweet nothings to each other throughout the whole ceremony and never took their eyes from one another.

Wells kept pulling on his mother's dress, trying to get her attention and eventually, they let him stand in front of her where he happily looked up at the pastor and asked "whattda doin'?"

In a matter of minutes, the pastor announced and presented Mr. and Mrs. Noah Litchfield to the congregation and the couple, with their son in their arms, walked out of the church to applause.

The limo brought them to The Veranda

where the guests had patiently waited for them to take the customary pictures at the church. The food was plenty, the wine and drinks were free flowing, the music outstanding and the guests had no problem awaiting their arrival. The new couple danced their shoes off and when it came time for the father-daughter dance, Kirkland graciously took Maddie's hand and waltzed her onto the dance floor. It was a moment she'd never forget.

As the night wore on, the toasts were made and the newlyweds made their way upstairs to change into their departure attire. They stopped just outside the door of the smaller ball room Simon had cordoned off for their personal use. Noah gathered Maddie up in his arms and kissed her long and softly. "I love you with all my heart," he whispered.

"I love you, too, and I'm so happy..." Maddie whispered back.

"Do you think they'll notice if we don't go back down?" Noah suggested, with a grin.

"Uh, yeah...I think they might."

"Yeah, it's just as well. If we get naked right now, we might miss our honeymoon all together."

"Speaking of, when are you going to tell me where we're going?" Maddie was beyond curious.

"When we get on the plane," Noah wasn't about to let it slip.

"Ugh...you know I had no idea how to pack. So I've had to pack a little of everything. Shorts, t-shirts, linen slacks, sandals, sweaters, scarves, wool slacks, boots...a woman really needs to know in advance."

"Never fear, my beautiful wife. Your dear friend Moby has unpacked what you won't need and even packed a few things you didn't know you'd need," Noah confessed.

"You let me pack all of that crap, just to have Moby unpack it all and start over?" she asked incredulously. "And Moby knows where we're going? *Heffa...* I even asked her if she knew and she denied knowing *anything.*"

"There is no limit to what I will do in order to surprise you...you don't know that by now?" Noah sheepishly said.

They quickly changed their clothes while stealing away a kiss here, a hug there, and a grope thrown in for good measure and headed back to their guests. Wells met them as they entered the grand ball room with a handful of wedding cake in one hand and a crab cake in the other.

"Ma ma.......cake! Da da....cake!" He squealed. Noah lifted his son into his arms. "I see you've got cake and then some, little one. How 'bout giving Mommy some?" Wells giggled and tried to push the cake into Maddie's mouth.

"Oh, no, you don't, rascal. That's Daddy's cake...." With that, Wells tried to feed the cake to Noah, laughing so hard he was bent over his father's arm. Sadie came up then and scooped the boy from Noah's arms.

"A E....cake! Cake....A E!!", he giggled and squirmed. Sadie laughed out loud and tried to wipe the child's mouth.

"Lawd amighty, dis hare boy done got hima mess! Come hare, now liddle un an let A E clean ya up..." She and Wells headed off to the kitchen to retrieve a wet towel.

****

Another hour passed and finally Noah and Maddie were wished farewells as the limo took them to the ferry. They had said goodbye to their family and friends and slathered Wells with kisses and hugs. Noah told him to be a good boy and mind his Meme and Popa and Maddie had cried when he kissed her square on the mouth and said "Wewws wuvs Ma ma." She didn't know how she'd stand to be away from him for two whole weeks.

Jestine and Kirkland, as well as Moby and Julia, had promised to show him pictures and videos of his parents while they were gone so he wouldn't forget them. And Maddie and Noah knew they'd call home every day to speak to him so he wouldn't forget their voices.

The limo didn't take them in the direction of the Charleston or Columbia airports and Maddie was confused. Instead it headed straight back into the Cope and headed for the small, private airport.

"Baby, I thought we were going by plane?"

she asked.

"We are. I just didn't say what plane," Noah smiled at his new wife.

"What?"

"We're going by private jet..." Noah grinned.

"What on earth?" Maddie gasped.

"Well, the old man has retired. He's got money to spend. He and Mother want to travel, but don't want the haggles of commercial flying, so he bought a private plane," Noah explained. "And it's our disposal, whenever, wherever, as long as he and Mother aren't using it."

"You've got to be kidding me....if my parents could only see me now!" Maddie exclaimed, grinning from ear to ear.

"Besides, if Wells needs us, we can get right back on this plane and come straight home. We don't have to wait on a flight back."

They arrived at the private air strip and were escorted onto the plane to find champagne, strawberries and an array of other treats awaiting them. The luggage was stored on the plane and as they buckled in, side by side, for takeoff, Maddie couldn't stand it any longer.

"Now will you tell me where we're going?" she asked.

"Not till we're in the air, the captain says we can get out of these seat belts and I can hold you in my arms."

Fifteen minutes later, the captain announced they were free to move about the cabin and Noah stood and took Maddie in his arms. Together they walked to a window and watched the moon dance across the Atlantic as they cut through the clouds.

"You know, doc," he whispered as he held her tightly, "you told me I should have gone to Paris for Christmas with my family."

"Yeah, I remember..." Maddie whispered back.

"Well, I'm going now....with my wife."

Maddie gasped and looked up at her husband. "Paris? We're going to Paris?"

"Yeah, baby....I'm taking you to Paris and not to stay in some hotel either. We've got our own little chateau overlooking the mountains, full maid and butler service and we're going to live like royalty for two whole weeks."

"Are we going to see all the sights, too? I mean, I've read about so many places I want to see, historical sites, museums, exhibits...there's so much I wanna see," Maddie was like a child.

Sweet Dreams, Doc

"Doc, we're going to see it all.....that is if we ever get out of bed." And they kissed. When the plane landed hours later, they were still kissing.

EPILOGUE

Wells was so excited, he was about to burst. His first day of four year old kindergarten was this morning and he had his 'book bag' packed full of writing tablets, big pencils and crayons. Maddie was trying in vain to get him to eat his eggs and grits and in between messy mouthfuls, he was rambling.

"Mommy, I go to big school today, wight?"

"Yes, little one, you're going to big school today. But not before you finish those grits. Would you like some more orange juice, baby?" Maddie asked, tousling his curly, chestnut hair.

He was already shaking that head full of curls. "Uh-uh, no fanks, I good for now," Wells replied with a mouthful of eggs.

Noah chuckled, "Alright, little man, don't be

talking with your mouth full..."

Wells laughed out loud displaying a mouth full of white teeth and a tongue full of chewed egg bits and grains of buttery grits. "I go to school wike Kuk and Mawy Gwace. I a big boy now, Daddy!" Maddie and Noah just giggled. "I got cwayons and papah and big, wed pencils...Mommy eben got me a peanut butter and jewwy sandwich and a juice box in my book bag for wecess..."

On and on he talked until finally they had his face cleaned and in the car headed to school. With camera in hand, Maddie watched as Noah led Wells by the hand into his first classroom. After several pictures and speaking with his teacher briefly, they promised him they would be right outside the school door at noon sharp to pick him up.

Whatever worries they had about separation anxiety upon being left there, Wells put to rest when he gave them both a hug and a kiss goodbye and turned to leave them with no second thoughts. Just as they reached the classroom door though, Wells let out a loud, “Mommy! Wait!!” He ran up to Maddie and wrapped his little arms around her legs and laid his head on her swollen belly, planting a tiny kiss on his soon-to-be born sister’s head. “Bye bye, Wiwwi...I wub you...”

Maddie wobbled down the school steps with tears in her eyes. Noah took her hand and helped her back to the car. When they were buckled in and headed back to the cottage, they both let out a collective sigh.

Noah squeezed Maddie’s hand and gently ran his thumb in circles around her palm. “He’s going to be fine, you know.”

Maddie wiped the tears from her eyes. “I know he will be. It’s just the hormones and all, of course, he's going to be fine. He's just grown up so fast. Where did the time go?"

"Well, doc, we've spent the last four years living and loving and being extremely happy. Making babies." He laid his hand softly on Maddie's pregnant belly. "It happens, you know, time keeps moving forward and look where we are now. We married off Julia and Hamp, then Moby and Clint. And look what we got outa that deal? Season tickets to the 'Dogs games. That was one sweet deal!"

"I love you, Noah. And I love our life together...it's gone by so fast, yet I can't believe in this short of time we've come so far."

"I have a surprise for you. At the house. I just hope it doesn't cause you to go into labor," Noah confessed with a grin.

"Really? You're not putting me on a plane somewhere are you? I know you and your surprises. Considering I'm already a week overdue, I hope whatever it is kicks me right into labor. I'm ready to get this girl here and outa me...." Maddie rested her head on the head rest.

Noah laughed a little. "No, I'm not putting you on a plane. And I seriously doubt if it's going to send you to the hospital, either."

Maddie poked out her bottom lip and mumbled, "Damn.."

They walked in the house and Noah led Maddie to the overstuffed sofa in the den and had her comfortably seated. He walked down to his office at the harbor and soon joined her on the sofa. He had an envelope in his hand and he handed it to her.

"Maddie, before you open that, I want to tell you something. You remember our first Christmas together, in Charleston?" Maddie nodded her head.

"You showed me your home, where you were raised and the property you decided to keep?" Again, she nodded. "We talked about one day building a vacation home on the remaining property, remember?"

"I remember," Maddie smiled. "I hope one day we can."

"Open the envelope, doc. I think this might be better than building a vacation home." Noah motioned for her to look inside the envelope. Maddie opened the clip on the manila envelope and removed some papers. She quickly realized she was holding a deed to a property in Charleston. Her eyes grew bigger when she realized what she was actually holding.

"Noah? What is this?"

"It's the deed to your parents house."

Maddie could barely speak. "It's what?"

"Baby, it's the deed to your parents' house. The house you grew up in. I bought it."

"You bought it? How? Why? I...can't..." Maddie was stumbling on her own thoughts and words.

"I found out through a friend of mine the folks that bought the place had decided to sell it. I knew right away I wanted to buy it, I took their decision to sell as a sign. I made them a handsome offer and they took it."

Maddie was crying so hard, she couldn't speak clearly. "Noah, I can't believe you did this. How did you know how much this would mean to me?"

"Because I know you. And you mean that much to me." He wrapped his arms around her. "I've had that deed for a whole week now and couldn't decide when to tell you. This morning you were so glum about Wells going to school, I thought it was a good time. Did it cheer you up?" Noah asked, already knowing the answer.

"I wish Moma and Daddy were here to see this. They wouldn't believe it! We actually have their home...for keeps. I never could quite accept the fact that strange people were going to be living in it....and now," she kissed Noah and put her hands on his face, "I won't ever have to."

"Well, the house needs a lot of work. The people hadn't lived in it for over a year and they hadn't done much to it while they were there. But I figured once the baby was born and you were back on your feet, it would be a good little weekend project for us. We can spend some long weekends there and you've got free reign on its renovation. I've already got a contractor committed to do the work, so it's all ready to go when you are."

"Oh, Noah. We'll make it a show place.

We'll do everything my parents always wanted to do with it and couldn't. And it'll be *ours*."

TWO DAYS LATER:

Maddie was pushing harder with each contraction. Beads of sweat were pooled on her forehead and blood vessels were already popping in her arms as she pulled on the stirrup handles.

Noah was so afraid for her, but showing no signs of it as he counted, "one, baby, two...come on, that's it, three, four, five....almost there now...."

The waiting room was full with Kirkland and Jestine, Julia and Hamp, Moby and Clint, little Wells, Julian, Celeste and the kids, even Sadie and Jasper all pacing back and forth and waiting for Noah to appear with the good news. Maddie had gone into labor early that morning and Wells had missed his third day of school in order to welcome his little sister into the world. Maddie progressed nicely and was in just her forty-fifth minute of pushing.

The doctor told her this would be her last push. "Alright, Maddie, your little girl is ready and this is it. I need one more really good push and it'll be over, okay?"

Maddie nodded and readied herself for the impending contraction. With one final struggle, their baby girl was born. All seven pounds of her and screaming her head off. Noah cut the cord and accepted his daughter into his waiting arms. He was crying again, as was Maddie, and he couldn't help but repeat to himself over and over, *'I have a daughter, I have a daughter...'*

He kissed Maddie on the mouth and handed the baby to the nurse. "I'll be right back, baby. I've got to let everyone know. Don't go anywhere..." he smiled and kissed her again.

He walked into the waiting room and everyone jumped to their feet. "She's here! And she is beautiful! She's looks just like Maddie," Noah announced proudly. Wells jumped into his daddy's arms and squealed..."yeahhhhhh!"

Noah hugged Wells tightly and told him, "Your mommy did good, little one and your sister can't wait to see you..."

Once everyone stopped asking a thousand questions, Noah shook his head. "Okay, okay, one at a time. She weighs seven pounds, is 19 inches long and her name is Lillian Austin Litchfield, after Maddie's parents. And we're calling her Lilli." He hugged everyone and told them Maddie was doing great, but he wanted to get back to her. He handed Wells over to Moby and left them to celebrate.

Maddie was resting quietly in her cleaned

bed when Noah returned. Lilli was still down in the nursery having all the regular testing done and the nurses had advised them she was perfectly normal and would be back to them soon. Noah gently climbed into the bed beside Maddie and took her into his arms.

"You did good, doc," he whispered.

"We did good..." she replied, with a sleepy smile.

"You okay? Are you hurting much? I know it was pretty bad."

"I'm good, baby...just tired." Maddie could hardly keep her eyes open. Noah pulled her closer and kissed her softly on the mouth.

"Close your eyes then, baby. I'm not leaving you. Get some sleep and I'll be right here when you wake up."

Maddie barely whispered "okay" before she

was sleeping soundly in his warm, loving embrace.

Noah kissed her forehead and gathered the blankets around her. He whispered ever so softly in her ear as she dozed off, “Sweet dreams, doc.”

THE END

Sweet Dreams, Doc

ABOUT THE AUTHOR:

Sheri is the single mom of two boys, Evan and Ethan…both of whom have given her precious grandchildren. She lives in the Lowcountry of South Carolina and finds her most peaceful moments at Edisto Beach. Her only true love of anything beyond her sons, grandchildren, friends and family are South Carolina's state reptile – the loggerhead sea turtle. She devotes most of her free time to the conservation and protection of these endangered creatures. She is lovingly called "The Turtle Lady" by the children of her community. She says "I have learned that family isn't always the one you're born into…it's the people you choose to spend your life with that make them "family." I have the best of both. It's all about living the life you were meant to live – the good days, the bad days and the fantastic days – life is too short to be anything but happy."

Made in the USA
Middletown, DE
04 September 2016